FINDING LOVE AT THE FOREVER HOME ON MUDDYPUDDLE LANE

Heart-warming, uplifting romance

Etti Summers

CHAPTER ONE

THE BALL OF FUR lay curled and quivering in the corner of the kennel, and Jakob wanted to cry. It broke his heart whenever he saw a dog who was so shut down that it seemed to have lost the will to live. This little scrap didn't even lift her head when he opened the door, the acknowledgement of his presence a mere flicker of her eye. He couldn't tell whether she was paralysed by fear or despondency. Both, probably.

'She isn't doing so well, is she?'

The woman's voice came from behind, and Jakob glanced over his shoulder and pulled a face. 'Some dogs can't handle being in kennels. She needs to be fostered.'

'I wish I could have her in the house with me.'

'They can't all live with *you*, Maisie. *I'll* foster her.'

Maisie Fairfax already had a houseful, having taken in a whippet bitch and her newborn puppies, and it was imperative that the pups weren't exposed to other dogs in the shelter until they were fully vaccinated.

She said, 'What about your two? Won't they mind?'

'They'll be fine.' Jakob had an elderly golden retriever named Stan, and a Bichon crossed with something unidentifiable called Ripley. Both were rescue dogs, obviously.

Not moving from his position near the door, Jakob crouched down, aware how threatening his bulk and height could be for something so small, and his heart spasmed when the dog flinched at the movement.

'Have you discovered anything more about her history?' Maisie asked.

Jakob shook his head. A member of the public had brought the dog in after finding her tied to railings in the park. Thin and terrified, her fur matted and dirty, she'd cowered, wide-eyed and shivering, as the vet had checked her over. No microchip, which wasn't a surprise, but no obvious infections or injuries, thank heaven.

Now that she'd had a bath and a trim, he thought she might have some Norfolk terrier in her because of her wiry tan coat and floppy ears. Physically, she was okay.

Mentally, she wasn't doing too good. He knew Maisie was doing her best, but she had other dogs to see to, and a business to run.

Maisie had recently opened The Forever Home Boarding Kennel on the mountain above the pretty village of Picklewick. She was kindly helping Thornbury Animal Sanctuary by letting them use part of the kennels, because the sanctuary was awash with unwanted and abandoned dogs.

Jakob had been reassigned to The Forever Home for the duration. This morning, he'd already cleaned five of the six kennels, fed the occupants, and checked them over. Soon he'd take each dog for one of its twice daily walks and continue with their training and assessments.

But, at the moment, his focus was on Trixie. He had no idea what the dog's name had been prior to her arrival at the sanctuary, so he'd named her Trixie.

'I'm going to sit with her for a bit,' Jakob said, hoping Maisie would take the hint and leave him be.

He liked the woman – as much as he liked anyone – but there was only so much peopling he could do and after chatting to her boyfriend, Adam, earlier, Jakob was all peopled out for a while. He needed to recharge his social battery, and the only way he knew how to do that was to be alone with a dog.

Right now, this one needed all his attention, so with his eyes on the scrap of fur in the corner, Jakob began the slow process of helping Trixie learn to love and trust again.

IF IT WASN'T NEXT door's dog howling, it was Zaza mewing, and between the two of them Gretta couldn't concentrate. And don't get her started on the birds. It was spring and they were nesting for all they were worth, creating so much noise that she had to keep the windows shut, despite it being such a lovely day.

With an exasperated sigh, she saved the newsletter she was working on, pushed her chair away from the desk and got to her feet.

The cat was sitting in the doorway to the small office, staring at her with big, chartreuse eyes. Gretta knew Zaza wanted one of two things – food or attention – and since she'd already had her breakfast, the cat probably wanted to be petted. Or *'worshipped'* as Zaza saw it.

Now that she'd got her subject's attention, Queen Zaza let out a chirp and strolled nonchalantly across the room, her fluffy grey tail upright and ramrod straight, the bell on her pink diamante collar tinkling.

Gretta knelt on the floor and stroked her fingers through the Persian's long fluffy fur, as Zaza arched her back and purred with contentment. But when another mournful howl rent the air, the cat scowled.

Zaza had one of those feline faces that looked perpetually cross at the best of times, but she could also give a pretty good scowl when she was particularly displeased.

'Is that nasty dog bothering you, sweetie? He's bothering me, too. Shall we go tell it to shut up?'

The noise had been going on all morning and Gretta was heartily sick of it. The dog didn't usually make a racket, not like *this*. It would bark when someone knocked on Mr Butler's door, or when it spotted Zaza on the fence separating the two gardens, and it would sometimes yelp to be let in if Mr Butler had forgotten it was outside. But this howling was unearthly.

The old man must have gone out, Gretta thought, although it was rare for him to leave the dog for long. If he wanted something from the village, he usually took it with him. She often saw him, hunched into an overcoat, the little dog by his side.

Aaawooohooo...

Zaza arched her back and hissed, and Gretta scrambled to her feet. Right, that's it! She'd have to go round there and tell him his dog was howling. She knew Mr Butler was deaf, but she didn't realise he was *that* deaf.

She pushed her chair back under the desk and made sure her work surface was tidy. After she'd given the old man a piece of her mind, she'd have an early lunch. She may as well since her concentration had been broken, then she'd resume work after she'd eaten. She could do with a break and a stretch of the legs anyway, because she'd been hard at it since seven this morning.

That was the beauty of being her own boss and working from home; as long as the work was done, she could please herself as to when. Sometimes, if she couldn't sleep, she worked at night. It helped keep those unwanted memories at bay, the ones that always seemed to rear their ugly heads in the middle of the night.

Gretta left her office (which was technically the third bedroom of her terraced house) and trotted downstairs, Zaza padding behind, but the cat hesitated when she saw Gretta remove her slippers and place them neatly by the front door. Zaza wouldn't follow her into the street. She preferred prowling around the gardens and the field behind the house. She didn't care for the road, which Gretta was thankful for. If anything happened to her cat, Gretta didn't know what she'd do. Zaza had been with her from the start of her new life in Picklewick. The cat was more than a companion: Zaza symbolised *freedom.*

Swapping the slippers for a pair of pumps, Gretta slid her mobile into her pocket and grabbed her keys, making sure to lock the front door behind her, even though she was only popping next door and even though she wouldn't be out of sight of it for even a second.

Automatically and without really realising she was doing it, Gretta glanced up and down the street. There wasn't a soul in sight, apart from the postman. He was heading away from her house, so she safely assumed he hadn't anything for her today.

Mr Butler didn't have a doorbell. He had an old-fashioned brass knocker: a very *loud* knocker. Its rat-a-tat sound sometimes made her jump, as it seemed to reverberate through the wall if she was in the living room. He didn't get many visitors though, she reflected, as she raised the knocker and let it fall.

Aaawooohooo...

Gretta shuddered. What was wrong with the dratted thing for it to make such a noise?

The wolf-like howl was immediately followed by a volley of yapping barks that faded away into silence as she waited on the doorstep.

Typical; Mr Butler wasn't in. *Or was he?* Was that music she could hear?

Gretta bent forward and hesitantly opened the letterbox flap. The music was instantly louder and she recognised it as the theme tune to one of the morning programmes on TV.

Exasperated, she dropped the flap, eliciting more barking, and banged on the knocker again.

The door remained stubbornly closed.

Unease stirred inside her, and she froze, her hand on the knocker. She had a feeling that something was amiss.

Gretta stepped back from the door and glanced at the window. The houses on this street didn't have front gardens; nothing stood between them and the pavement, so with another glance up and down the road, Gretta walked over to her neighbour's living room window.

Cupping her hands around her eyes, she peered through it, trying to see beyond the yellowing net curtain.

Was that—?

Oh, hell, it *was!* The poor man!

Mr Butler was lying on the floor and he didn't appear to be moving. His little black and white dog sat next to him, staring up at the window.

Gretta stumbled back, reaching for her phone, and as she did, the howling started again. The dog obviously thought she was abandoning him and his master.

As she rang for an ambulance, she tried the handle, fully expecting the front door to be locked, and was surprised to discover that it wasn't.

'Is the patient breathing?' the operator asked.

'Hang on, I'm going in now,' Gretta said, hurrying inside. The howling turned to whimpering, and a skitter of claws on the lino in the hall made her hesitate. Was the dog friendly? Might it attack her?

She flinched as it launched itself at her, then realised its back end was waggling as it jumped up at her legs.

Gretta ignored it and hastened to Mr Butler's side.

His eyes were closed. Tentatively she reached out and pressed two fingers against the side of his neck. She thought she felt a pulse, but she wasn't entirely sure because she was shaking so much.

'Is the patient breathing?' the operator repeated.

Gretta scrutinised Mr Butler's chest and was relieved to see a shallow rising and falling. 'Yes.'

'Is the patient conscious?'

She shook him gently. 'Mr Butler, can you hear me? Mr Butler?' There was no response. 'No, he isn't.'

'Keep talking to him. An ambulance will be with you shortly.'

Wishing the operator had stayed on the line, Gretta hurried to the front door to open it, then dashed back to the old man; she'd sit with him until help arrived.

The dog was lying next to him, licking his face, and she grimaced. 'Shoo!' She waved a hand at it.

The animal ignored her. It carried on licking its master, a low whine issuing from its throat.

Gretta decided to leave him be. Mr Butler had more than dog saliva to worry about. His skin had a deathly pallor and his lips were purple, bordering on blue. Heart trouble?

Mindful of the operator's advice, she said, 'It's Gretta, from next door. Don't worry, help is on its way. You'll be okay, Mr Butler. The hospital will sort you out.'

He must have heard her, her presence registering on some level, because he stirred, his eyelids fluttering, his mouth working. His breathing deepened and he hitched in a rattling breath. The exhalation carried a wheezing whisper.

'Don't try to speak,' she told him. 'Save your strength. The ambulance will be here any minute.' God, she hoped that was true.

The dog whined again, the sound piteous, and it tried to squirm closer. Gretta pushed it away, but it scrabbled back into position.

'Bertie.' The word was faint, barely a whisper.

'I'll put him in the kitchen, shall I?' she suggested. The last thing the paramedics needed was a dog getting in the way.

'No.' The old man grasped her arm with surprising strength. 'Promise me.'

'Promise you what, Mr Butler?'

He said something, but she didn't catch it, so she shuffled nearer and bent her head, her ear close to his mouth. 'Can you say that again?'

'Bertie…promise me…you'll look after him.' His mouth dropped open as he gasped for breath.

'Oh, I'm not… I don't know…' The request caught her unawares.

'Please. Tell him I love him.'

'Tell who?'

'*Bertie.* Look after him.' The old man's eyelids opened, revealing cloudy, panicked eyes, and the grip on her arm tightened. '*Please.*'

'Of course I will,' she assured him reluctantly. What else could she say?

'Promise?' His voice was urgent.

'I promise.' It wasn't a hard promise to make. After all, it would only be for a few hours. Maybe for the rest of the day, if Mr Butler was kept in overnight. Someone would turn up to take it off her hands. She'd pop in a couple of times to check on it until they did.

To her relief, noise and a flurry of activity alerted her to the arrival of the paramedics.

Worried that the dog might panic and bolt, she scooped up the solid little body and deposited the pooch in the kitchen, shutting the door firmly. The howling began immediately.

Gretta wanted to yell at it to shut up but was conscious that if it hadn't been for the racket the dog had made, she would never have found Mr Butler. He might have lain on his lounge floor for hours. Days. It didn't bear thinking about.

But long after the ambulance had taken Mr Butler away, it was all Gretta *was* able to think about.

THE DOG HADN'T shut up. It had barked and whimpered the whole time the paramedics had been there, carrying on when Gretta returned home. She'd left it in Mr Butler's kitchen, after checking that it had food and water and hadn't needed to go out for a wee. However, that had been over two hours ago, and the noise hadn't stopped.

Gretta had to admire the little creature's stamina. It was a wonder it hadn't given itself a sore throat. Could dogs get sore throats, she wondered, sighing in irritation: she couldn't remember whether she'd sent a draft copy of the newsletter to the author in question and now had to go back into the programme to check.

She *had* sent it, she discovered crossly, and as soon as the author gave her the okay, she would email it to the woman's many thousands of subscribers.

Gretta was a virtual personal assistant to several authors, performing a variety of tasks including managing social media accounts, updating websites, marketing, and creating newsletters. Some authors wanted her to do all the things that a writer had to do (apart from actually *writing* the book) and others wanted a reduced service, such as content creation for blog posts. It was varied and interesting work and Gretta loved it, especially since it played to her excellent organisational skills.

Aaawooohooo...

Gretta slapped her palm on the desk in irritation. This couldn't go on. Goodness knows how long it would be before someone came to see to the dratted thing. It could be hours yet, and she still had a considerable amount of work to do before she wanted to finish for the day.

After accessing the online project planning software, Gretta updated the author's task sheet with the newsletter details. It was imperative that everything was dated and documented, otherwise how could she keep track? It was also imperative that she was able to concentrate and when the howling turned to barking, Gretta flinched. She didn't know which was worse.

What she did know was that she wanted it to stop. She would have to go round there, she decided. Maybe it needed another garden visit?

Swapping her slippers for the shoes in the hall, she checked she had Mr Butler's key. It had been in the lock, on the inside of his front door, and she'd taken it with her after he'd been bundled into the ambulance, not wanting to leave his property unlocked. She'd give it to whoever came to see to the dog. Having it in her possession made her uncomfortable. She didn't want the responsibility.

The noise briefly stopped when she entered his house, resuming in earnest before she'd taken more than a couple of steps into the hall, the timbre of the barks changing from despondent to excitement, then on reaching the kitchen, she could hear whimpering and scrabbling as he clawed at the door. But when she opened it, all noise ceased as the dog realised she wasn't who he was hoping for.

'Sorry, Bertie, it's me, Gretta, from next door.'

The dog backed away and sat on his haunches, regarding her solemnly.

Gretta was grateful for the silence. 'Do you need to go out?' She unlocked the door to the garden and pushed it open.

The dog continued to stare at her and didn't move.

'No? What then?' He hadn't touched his food, and his water bowl was still half full so he couldn't be hungry or thirsty. 'Are you missing your owner? Is that it?'

Bertie blinked at her.

'Shall we see how he is, eh? What if I give the hospital a call?'

The dog wouldn't understand, but she was rather concerned. The old man hadn't looked well, and the expression on the paramedics' faces had been grim.

She found the number for Thornbury General, then spent ages being passed from department to department. While she was waiting, she pulled out a chair at the Formica-topped table and sat down. Bertie, she noticed, came forward for a sniff, then promptly plonked his backside down on her foot. He was a warm, solid weight, staring up at her with mournful eyes.

'It'll be alright,' she told him.

But when she finally got through to someone who could tell her how Bertie's owner was, the news wasn't good.

Mr Butler was dead.

CHAPTER TWO

A LOUD RAT-A-TAT made Gretta yelp in surprise and set Bertie off again. He scrambled past her, his claws clattering on the lino, and dashed into the hall.

Gretta got to her feet, relieved that her dog-sitting duty was at an end.

It wasn't until she saw who was on the step that the anomaly struck her: a relative of Mr Butler wouldn't be ringing the doorbell because they'd know he wasn't here.

It was Harriet Brown from two doors up – two doors from Gretta, that is. Harriet (call me Hattie) lived on Mr Butler's other side.

'Is he in?' Harriet demanded. 'I want a word about his bloody dog. I take it you're here for the same reason?'

'No, actually—'

'For goodness' sake, get down!' Bertie was on his hind legs, front paws scrabbling at Harriet's knees. 'Tell Mr Butler from me, that if he can't keep the bloody thing quiet, I'm phoning the police.'

'He's dead.'

'Pardon?'

'Mr Butler died this morning.'

Harriet's irate expression changed instantly.

'Oh, the poor man. How did he—? Was it a—?'

'I don't know the details. I found him collapsed on the floor when I came to talk to him about the dog barking. I'm surprised you didn't see the ambulance.'

Harriet looked cross that she'd missed it. 'I had to pop out.' She narrowed her eyes. 'If it happened this morning, why has the dog been barking all afternoon? And why are *you* still here?' This last was said with a degree of suspicion.

'Mr Butler asked me to look after him. I was hoping you were a relative. I can't keep popping back and forth every five minutes to see to him.'

'You can't let it bark all the time. The noise goes right through you, it's that loud.'

'Could you take him? I can't – I've got a cat.'

'*Me?* No chance. My hubby's allergic. Can't you hang onto it until someone shows up?' She peered past Gretta, her eyes darting around the hall. 'The vultures will soon be here, mark my words.'

'Do you know who they might be? Did he have any children?'

'I don't think so. I believe there's a niece, or maybe not...' She trailed off and stared down at the dog.

Gretta followed her gaze. Bertie was sitting on his haunches, his sad face staring up at them, and she felt a twinge of sympathy for the little chap. He must be missing his owner dreadfully and was probably wondering what was going on.

Harriet said, 'Someone at the post office might know who Mr Butler's next of kin is.'

It was a good idea. After thanking her, Gretta ushered the dog inside the house and locked the door. She'd pop back later and—

Bertie began howling again, and Gretta gritted her teeth.

'Right, that's it,' Harriet announced. 'I'm calling the police. They can deal with it. I'm not prepared to listen to *that* for the rest of the day. And what if he keeps it up all night?'

Gretta was tempted to let Harriet call the police, but she'd made a promise and in all conscience she couldn't renege on it. Besides, she felt sorry for the old man. How would she feel if she wasn't able to look after Zaza, and her little darling was left all alone for hours on end? Besides, Gretta couldn't do that to the dog. There was nothing else for it – Bertie would have to stay with her for the duration.

Aware of Harriet glaring at her, Gretta hastily unlocked the door again, and the noise immediately ceased.

'There you have it,' Harriet announced in satisfaction. 'He'll have to stay with you until you find Mr Butler's next of kin. Either that, or...' She ground to a halt and waggled her eyebrows meaningfully.

Gretta wasn't keen on dogs, but she couldn't be that heartless.

With a sigh, she went back inside to fetch everything she thought the animal might need for an overnight stay and prayed it wouldn't be any longer than that. She'd drop him off at hers, then go to the post office and ask whether anyone had any information on Mr Butler's relations.

On second thoughts, she'd better take the dog with her, because she daren't leave him alone with Zaza.

Oh, gosh, *Zaza!*

The sooner Gretta could hand Bertie over to someone else, the better, because Zaza *was not* going to be pleased.

JAKOB WAS FORCED to carry Trixie. When he'd taken her out of the kennel, the little dog had stood there, refusing to move, her tail tucked under her tummy, her back hunched and her ears flattened to her head. And she'd quivered so violently, Jakob thought he could hear her teeth chattering.

The sooner he got her away from this situation and settled with him, the better. His two were used to having unexpected guests and wouldn't bat an eyelid. Hopefully, his pooches would be a reassuring and calming influence on the terrified dog.

Opening his estate car's rear door, he gently placed Trixie in a crate. He kept two permanently in the back, and both were well used because he took his dogs with him most places, except to work. They'd be delighted to see him when he got home, but first he wanted to nip into the village on the way for a few bits and bobs, and he had a parcel to send, so he'd do that at the same time.

He found a space on the high street and pulled in. The post office was a short walk away, as was the small convenience store, and he considered leaving Trixie in the car. But one look at her scared face made him decide to take her with him. She'd be okay tucked under his arm, plus he wanted her to get used to his scent and voice.

Speaking softly, he lifted her out of the crate, holding her with one arm, and his heart went out to her when she buried her nose in the crook of his neck.

'I know, sweetie,' he crooned. 'It's very scary, isn't it? You're safe, little one.'

As Jakob strode along the pavement, he noticed she'd gone into shut-down mode again, her body floppy, and he silently cursed whoever had allowed an innocent little creature to get into such a state. Some people shouldn't be permitted anywhere near animals, and certainly shouldn't be allowed to own something as loving and as sensitive as a dog. Some people—

Jakob's train of thought was derailed by the sight of a black and white French bulldog doing its business right outside the post office. Its owner, a pretty woman around thirty years old, wore a disgusted expression.

'Aren't you going to pick that up?' he demanded, as she began to walk away, the dog having finished.

She stopped. 'I, um...what with?' Now she looked embarrassed as well as disgusted.

And this had to happen just as he'd been thinking that some people, like *this one* for instance, shouldn't be allowed to own a dog, not if they weren't prepared to pick up after it and were happy to leave the mess in the middle of the pavement for anyone to step in.

'A poo bag?' He knew he was being sarcastic, but the silly woman deserved it.

The Frenchie jumped up at him, paws on his leg, and sniffed at Trixie, who stared at it lethargically. It was going to be a while before she came out of her shell.

The woman said, 'I don't have...I haven't...'

Annoyed, Jakob pulled a couple of bags out of his pocket. 'Here. And next time, bring some with you.' He ruffled her dog's ears, hoping the animal hadn't picked up on his irritation, but guessing that he probably had. 'There's a good boy,' he said, and received a lick on the hand in return.

'How do I—?' the woman began, stopped, then said, 'I don't have a scoop.'

'A *scoop?*' He barked out a laugh. 'It isn't an ice cream. It's dog sh—'

'I know what it is,' she snapped, interrupting him. Lifting her chin, she gave him a fierce glare. She had the most gorgeous hazel eyes, he thought distractedly, large and luminous with thick dark lashes.

Her expression haughty, she said, 'I have a cat. I use a scoop to clean out her litter tray.'

Jakob shook his head in disbelief. 'You bring a *scoop* out with you? *Why?*'

'No, you misunderstand me. I don't bring a scoop with me.'

'But you just said— Never mind!' His patience was growing thin. 'How do you usually pick up your dog's poop?'

'I don't.'

His mouth dropped open. 'What? *Never?* You're one of those dirty, disgusting peop—'

'This isn't my dog! I don't have a dog. I don't *want* a dog, but I seem to be saddled with one.'

'Ah. I see. In that case...' He took another poo-bag out of his pocket and dealt with the mess himself, with a bit of a flourish to show her how it was done.

The woman looked horrified and Jakob chuckled. 'Haven't you seen anyone pick up dog poo before?'

'It's not something I take any interest in.' Her reply was lofty.

'If he goes again, that's how you do it,' he explained.

'He won't, will he?' She looked down at the little dog anxiously.

'Hopefully not on *this* walk,' Jakob chortled. 'But I'm sure you understand how these things work: at some point he *will* go again.'

She closed her eyes. It was brief, but it gave Jakob the opportunity to look at her properly. She was considerably shorter than him (but then, most people were) and curvy, with dark hair falling to her shoulders and an elfin face with a generous mouth.

When she opened her eyes again, her gaze landed on the poo bag he was still holding. She looked a little green around the gills.

'Would you like me to dispose of this for you?' he asked, surprising himself. He wasn't usually this accommodating. Or chatty.

'Would you mind?'

He shrugged.

'Thank you, I appreciate it.'

He shrugged again, suddenly all out of conversation. He was done with people for today.

Conscious of the need to go home and get Trixie settled in, he walked away, not giving a single hoot that the woman might think him rude. What people thought didn't concern him.

But when he reached the bin, he couldn't help glancing back – at the dog, naturally.

Or that's what he told himself.

ZAZA TOOK ONE look at the intruder and fled. Bertie, possibly unable to believe his luck at finding a cat so close, gave chase. Fortunately for Zaza, he was still on the lead. Unfortunately for Gretta, he was stronger than he looked and, caught unawares, she was yanked forward, lost her balance and fell, sprawling the length of the hall. Thankfully, she kept hold of the lead.

As she lay there cursing, her arm being pulled out of its socket by a yipping, lunging ball of excitement, Gretta's compassion for Bertie began to wane. Clearly, looking after him in her house, even if only for a short time, wasn't going to work. But keeping him at his own wouldn't work, either.

At a loss and feeling frustrated, Gretta yelled, 'Will you behave!'

The result was instantaneous. Bertie froze. Then the lead went slack as he stopped pulling and turned to look at her with wary eyes.

'You don't like being shouted at? Tough, because I don't like you trying to yank my arm off.' She clambered to her feet and unwrapped the end of the lead from her hand, noticing the indents on the back of it where the leather had dug into her skin.

For such a small dog, the little blighter was unbelievably strong.

One thing was certain, she wasn't going to be able to let him off the lead any time soon – she couldn't risk him upsetting Zaza more than she already was – so the next few hours were going to be intolerable. She just hoped that Mr Butler's relatives wouldn't take long to arrive. Unfortunately, her enquiries at the post office hadn't yielded anything more than pity for Mr Butler and a general moan about funeral expenses.

If his next of kin hadn't put in an appearance by tomorrow, she'd phone the hospital again and ask whether they had any details.

Praying that she wouldn't have to look after Bertie overnight, Gretta ushered him into the kitchen. She'd leave him in there for a few minutes while she soothed Zaza's shredded nerves.

Gretta slipped the dog's lead under the leg of the table to anchor him in place, then closed the door on him.

The howling began immediately.

Gritting her teeth, she went in search of her cat, finding her hiding under her bed, fur fluffed up, tail like a bottle brush, and eyes flashing. Zaza was growling, almost vibrating with fury.

It took Gretta a while to coax her out. 'I won't let that nasty dog get you,' she promised, but from the way Zaza arched her back and puffed herself up even more, Gretta guessed her cat wasn't convinced. And no wonder, with all the noise coming from the kitchen.

Actually, she realised it had stopped a few minutes ago. That was a good sign, right?

Gretta left Zaza crouching uneasily on the bed, the cat looking considerably less cross but still on edge. Gretta knew how she felt...

And when she saw what Bertie had been up to in her absence, her stress levels soared. The little sod was still attached to the table, but he'd dragged it halfway across the room, close enough to get to the bin, whose contents were now strewn all over the floor.

Gretta recoiled in dismay.

The dog had his back to her and was busily nosing around in the rubbish, making little snuffling, grunting noises.

'Get away from there!' she cried and clapped her hands. Then she let out a shriek when she saw his face as he whirled around to look at her. The white parts of his fur were yellow, and the black bits weren't much better.

The dog was covered in fine yellow powder and so were his paws, and the rest of the kitchen would shortly be covered in it as well, she realised, as he lunged towards her. Fortunately, the lead he was still attached to brought him up short.

It was custard powder. She'd had her quarterly clear-out of the kitchen cupboards yesterday and had thrown out a tin because it was past its best-before date. Somehow the dog had got the plastic lid off.

For Pete's sake! Bertie had only been in her house for half an hour, and he'd already caused chaos. And now she was going to have to bath him, because how else would she get the yellow out of his fur!

Bertie's ears went down and his whole body drooped, as though he could read her mind. Then she realised it wasn't the bath that bothered him, it was his stomach, as he promptly threw up a mass of yellow slime.

Gross!

'BERTIE! *NOOO!*' Gretta wailed, as the dog scrambled out of the bath, slopping yellow-tinged sudsy water all over her and the floor. She was already wet from wrestling with him to get him in the bath and keep him there long enough to lather him up, and now she was utterly drenched.

Bertie, she'd discovered, wasn't keen on being bathed. And Gretta had discovered that *she* wasn't keen on the process, either.

'Agh!' she cried as he shook himself violently, his little ears flapping, his solid body rolling from side to side, the shake ending at his stumpy little tail as she tried to throw an old towel over him.

He wriggled out from underneath it, then clamped his jaws on a corner of the fabric and began to tug, issuing ferocious-sounding growls.

Alarmed, Gretta relinquished her grasp on the towel and threw herself backwards, frightened that Bertie was about to attack her.

Bertie, who had been tugging with all his might, slid on the wet floor and thudded into the side of the bath; he kept hold of the towel though, and when he regained his balance, he shook it with the same vigour a fox might shake a rat. The growls were frightening, but when she realised he was playing, Gretta's fear changed to outrage as she surveyed her once-pristine bathroom.

Gritting her teeth and gathering her resolve, she risked life and limb to grab the dog and heave him back into the bath, towel and all. Using one arm to hold him in place, Gretta aimed the shower head at him and rinsed the furry little body until the water ran clear.

Reaching for a dry towel, she draped it over him and lifted him out before he could leap out. Not that it would make any difference, because she was soaking anyway.

After drying him off as best she could, with much shaking from Bertie, Gretta turned her attention to the state of her bathroom, ignoring the dog, who was sliding around the floor, his face buried in a towel, his back legs propelling himself across the tiles. Leaving him to it (she wasn't entirely sure why he was doing that, but he seemed to be trying to dry himself) Gretta donned a pair of rubber gloves, grabbed a bottle of spray disinfectant and set to, cleaning up the mess.

When she was satisfied, she (very reluctantly) took the annoying little creature into the bedroom with her while she changed into clean, dry clothes, keeping a wary eye out for Zaza as she did so.

Gretta had just pulled her wet tee shirt over her head, when Bertie went ballistic, zooming around the room at a hundred miles an hour, leaping onto the bed and off again in manic circles. Cushions and pillows were scattered willy-nilly, as he scuffed her gorgeous bedspread into a rumpled heap.

'Stop!' she yelled at the top of her voice, appalled at the mess he was making.

Bertie ignored her, making several more laps before collapsing onto his tummy, his pink tongue lolling.

'Get off my bed *now!*' Gretta shouted, putting as much authority as she could into her voice.

Bertie stared at her but didn't move, so Gretta growled at him.

The dog blinked in surprise, then slunk off the bed, dropping onto the carpet with a thud and a grunt.

'Thank you.' Feeling self-conscious and wishing Bertie wouldn't stare at her, Gretta hastily changed into dry clothes.

Ready to tackle the kitchen (the thought made her shudder), Gretta ushered the dog downstairs, hoping Zaza had the sense to make herself scarce. The last thing she needed right now was another altercation.

Deciding that she didn't want Bertie under her feet while she tried to clean the kitchen and not trusting him to behave himself if she left him in the sitting room, Gretta shoved him out into the garden. It was fenced, so he should be safe enough out there.

Thirty-five minutes later, the kitchen was spotless and Gretta could finally relax. She'd feed Zaza, make herself a meal, then after she'd eaten, she'd do a couple of hours' work before bed. She was exhausted: it had been a trying day and—

She stopped in the middle of reaching for a pouch of cat food, suddenly remembering that there was a dog in her garden. A dog that it would appear she would have to look after overnight. A dog that she'd kind of forgotten about for the past half an hour. A dog that was covered in dirt, she discovered, when she opened the back door and Bertie shot past her, leaving a trail of muddy paw prints across her gleaming kitchen floor.

And when he gave himself a shake and spattered the newly cleaned units, Gretta promptly burst into tears. Not only did she have to clean the blasted kitchen for a second time, but the bloody dog would also need another bloody bath!

CHAPTER THREE

JAKOB KNEW IT WAS better to let Trixie find her own way and settle in her own time. Fussing her would only make her more anxious. Therefore, he did his utmost to ignore her and let her get on with it. It was hard, though.

Leaving her in the car for a moment while he went into the bungalow, he spent a few minutes greeting his excited dogs, and only when they'd calmed down sufficiently did he fetch Trixie.

He walked into the kitchen carrying her, his two following on his heels, staring up at the newcomer. Both Stan and Ripley were friendly, and it wasn't unusual for him to bring home a strange dog for a few days or weeks, so he didn't anticipate any issues from them.

Trixie, on the other hand, might be more suited to being an only dog, so despite pretending to ignore her after he placed her gently on the floor, he was actually keeping a very close eye on the situation.

Stan, being the gentleman that he was, hung back, his golden flag of a tail waving gently, his mouth open, tongue lolling. Ripley enthusiastically sniffed the stranger, while Trixie cowered, her tail between her legs, disliking the intrusion.

Knowing that Ripley would be easily distracted by food, Jakob began preparing their meals, immediately getting Ripley's attention as the dog sat at his feet, staring up at him intently and licking his lips, which gave Stan an opportunity to say hello to the newcomer by gently nosing her.

Trixie, bless her, looked terrified, but despite wanting to scoop her up and cuddle her, Jakob carried on measuring out the food into three bowls. He'd feed his two in the porch and put Trixie's bowl down in the kitchen so she could eat in peace. He didn't expect her to touch it though, guessing she'd be too anxious. If she didn't show any interest in it, he'd offer it to her again later, and he'd keep offering it to her until she felt settled enough to eat.

Jakob had just closed the porch door, leaving his two inside eagerly tucking into their tea, when his phone rang. It was Dawn, the manager of Thornbury Animal Sanctuary, checking in.

'I've brought that little terrier, Trixie, home with me,' he told her.

'I thought you might. Shall I see if I can find someone to foster her?'

Jakob shook his head before remembering she couldn't see him. 'It's okay. She can stay with me; I want to assess her anyway.' While he was updating his boss on the other residents of The Forever Home, Jakob kept an eye on Trixie, who had crept under the table.

As predicted, she hadn't shown any interest in her food, so after the phone call ended he picked up her bowl, then let his boys out. He'd have a bite to eat himself, before taking them for a walk. They'd already been out twice today – he'd walked them early in the morning before work and his parents had called in at midday to take them out again – but they'd happily go for another. Trixie would come too: exercise and a chance to have a good sniff would help calm her.

And *him.* Because, as he'd driven home, he'd caught sight of the woman who'd broken his heart, and to his dismay the pain had been as sharp as ever.

GRETTA CONSIDERED herself reasonably intelligent but she had no experience with dogs. Never owned one, never wanted to own one, and didn't know anyone who did. Even if she had known someone with a dog, she probably wouldn't ask them for advice.

She disliked being beholden to anyone. Besides, there weren't many people left who she could be beholden *to.* Landon had seen to that.

Not wanting to give her ex-partner any more headspace, Gretta busied herself by searching the internet for answers, although it was difficult to concentrate when there was a restless dog wandering around her feet.

She'd been forced to take Bertie upstairs with her, despite abhorring the thought of the dog in her office, because she simply couldn't trust him. And neither could she cope with the unbearable noise whenever she tried to leave him on his own. Even nipping to the loo had been a trial, she'd discovered, when she'd left him in the kitchen (with the now-empty bin) for five minutes. He'd howled the place down.

Gretta was now dreading going to bed. Which was why she was in her office, sitting at her desk and feeling very despondent. Having managed to eliminate one incredibly controlling and domineering male from her life, it seemed she'd acquired another, albeit a much smaller one. Hopefully this one wouldn't be around for more than a day or so.

After half an hour of learning more about dogs than she'd ever wanted to know, Gretta was none the wiser. Her predicament was unusual, she concluded, because the majority of references to barking and howling dogs were aimed at people who already owned the animal, or who had just acquired a puppy and were trying to persuade it to settle on its own without its mother or littermates. None mentioned how to cope with a dog you were only looking after for a few hours.

Giving up, she got to her feet, Bertie following.

Momentarily forgetting why her office door was shut, Gretta opened it to find Zaza on the other side.

Both animals froze.

Then pandemonium broke out.

Zaza, wide-eyed and panicked, fled into Gretta's bedroom. Bertie let out a yip of excitement and immediately gave chase, bolting after the cat in a blur of black and white.

Gretta let out a scream and dived across the landing in a flying rugby tackle that missed Bertie completely, to land flat on her face with her arms outstretched. She lay there, stunned. But not for long, as her petrified cat bolted out of the bedroom to briefly alight on her back, dig her claws in and use Gretta's spine as a springboard to launch herself down the stairs.

'Ow!' Gretta yelped, but before she could move, fifteen kilos of dog scrambled over her, flattening her completely and grinding her nose into the carpet.

'Bertie!' she shrieked, her cry losing some of its volume as the sound was muffled by the cream shag pile. It was also lost in the din coming from downstairs: frantic barking and high-pitched yowling, along with crashes and thuds.

Oh, God! If he hurt Zaza, Gretta wouldn't be responsible for her actions!

She clambered to her feet and dashed for the stairs, lurching from wall to wall as she staggered down them and almost fell into the living room, her heart in her mouth.

Then halted abruptly at the sight that greeted her.

One of the armchairs was tipped over backwards, her bookcase was upended, and the table in the corner lay on its side. Books and cushions were scattered all over the floor, and one end of the curtain pole had come away from the wall. Zaza was clinging to the top of the other end, peering down at Bertie, who had the curtain in his mouth and was tugging it with all his might, trying to dislodge the cat.

Zaza's tail lashed back and forth, savage growls issuing from deep in her throat, alternating between threatening hisses. She must have been aiming for the partially open living room window but hadn't yet managed to slip through it much to Gretta's relief, because it was directly on the road and although the street was a relatively quiet one, there was still too much traffic for Gretta's liking.

'Bertie!' Gretta's shriek was loud enough and high enough to shatter glass.

Bertie froze, his hindquarters bunched underneath him, the hem of the curtain in his mouth. He turned his head, his eyes swivelling towards her, and without moving any other part of him, he let go of the fabric. Slowly his ears came up, then drooped when he saw her appalled expression.

'That's it! I've had enough. I don't care if you howl all night, I'm taking you home.' Furious and near to tears, she stomped towards him.

Bertie cowered, whining as she picked him up.

'It's no good crying now,' she scolded. 'It's too late. Actions have consequences. I can't have you terrorising Zaza.' She gazed up at her cat.

Zaza spat at him, her eyes flashing sparks. Her fur was so puffy, she looked twice her normal size.

Gretta, distressed and angry, tightened her hold on the dog and marched to the front door, but before she could open it the bell rang, and she hesitated.

She wasn't expecting anyone. None of her family lived near enough to simply drop in on the off-chance and they wouldn't anyway since she didn't have much to do with them, and she'd lost touch with her friends a long time ago.

Wary now, she hoisted the dog into a more comfortable position, and sidled up to the spyhole, her spirits lifting as it occurred to her that it might be one of Mr Butler's relatives. After all, she *had* left a note asking them to fetch him as soon as possible.

Squinting, one eye closed, she peered through the tiny hole.

A police officer was on the other side.

With a gasp, Gretta tore her gaze away and took a step back. Her heart in her mouth, her pulse hammering, she gingerly unlocked the door.

'Miss Laverne?'

'Yes?' Her voice was a high-pitched squeak. A police officer at the door could only mean one thing. 'Is it my parents? One of my sisters? What's happened?'

'They're not the reason I'm here.' His eyes narrowed. 'Are you alright?'

'I'm fine.'

'Are you sure?'

'Yes.' She sagged against the doorframe. 'I thought you were the bearer of bad news.'

He was peering past her into the hall. 'Can I come in?'

'No!' Gretta was horrified. There was no way she was letting him see the state her sitting room was in, even if he was a police officer.

'You live here alone, don't you?' he asked.

'How do you know?'

'I live opposite.' He gestured to a house on the other side of the street. 'We're neighbours.' His attention turned to Bertie, who was squirming in her arms. 'Isn't that Mr Butler's dog? I'd heard he'd passed away.'

'Yes. Are you here about him? Have you found his next of kin?' Hope flared in her chest.

'Ah, no...I'm here because a disturbance was reported at this address.'

'*My address?*'

'Yes.' His eyes flickered to the window and she assumed he could see the dangling curtain pole and possibly the cat who was still perched on it. 'Actually,' he admitted, 'I forgot my sandwiches and popped back home for them. It was me who heard the disturbance. Are you *sure* you're alright?'

Some of Gretta's tension eased. It was nice of him to check on her. 'My cat had a run-in with Bertie,' she explained. 'He chased her around the living room and knocked over my bookcase, amongst other things.'

The officer was studying her, as though trying to determine whether she was telling the truth.

She added, 'I'm just about to take him home. I can't keep him here. The problem is, I'm worried he'll bark all night. I kind of feel responsible for him because I promised Mr Butler I'd look after him. I'm praying it won't be for long.' She bit her lip, then said, 'But what if it is? I can't have him in mine – he's a bloody menace.'

'Is there anyone else who—?'

'No one.' A thought occurred to her. 'Could the police take him?'

He shook his head. 'Sorry, no can do. You'll need to phone the council and ask for the dog warden. They can kennel him for up to seven days.'

Eyes wide, Gretta asked, 'What happens after seven days?'

'A re-homing centre, I believe.'

The officer *believed*, but he wasn't *certain*. She mightn't be enamoured with the creature, but she couldn't take the risk that anything untoward might happen to him if Mr Butler's nearest and dearest couldn't be found in that time.

Bertie whined, a pitiful sound, as though he understood that his future was being discussed.

With her arms aching (the dog, who was no stick insect, was getting heavier by the second) Gretta thanked the officer for his concern and she was about to go back inside when he said, 'You could try giving Maisie Fairfax a call. She owns The Forever Home Boarding Kennel on Muddypuddle Lane and has recently started taking in dogs for re-homing. I'm

Gio Alfonso, by the way. My partner, Nikki, is her sister.'

'Okay, thanks. I'll hang onto him for a day or so, see if anyone comes to collect him. And if not...' She left the rest of the sentence hanging, undecided. If she was honest, she wasn't sure she'd be able to manage to hang onto him for an hour, let alone a whole day.

Deciding not to take him next door after all, she returned to the living room to fetch his lead. She couldn't think why she'd removed it in the first place. If she'd had kept it on him, the 'disturbance' wouldn't have happened at all. Therefore, by Gretta's reasoning, if she didn't take Bertie's lead off except for when he was in the garden and doing his business, *this* – she scanned the living room – wouldn't occur again.

Zaza, she'd noticed, had descended from the curtain pole and was now perched on the back of the remaining upright chair, her fur still puffed up, her tail lashing. And when she saw Bertie in her owner's arms, she hissed vehemently, following it up with a growl in case the dog didn't take the hiss seriously.

'It's okay,' Gretta soothed. 'I've got him, and I won't let him anywhere near you again.'

Zaza's glare told Gretta that the cat didn't believe a word of it. Clipping the lead onto Bertie's harness, Gretta put him down with a relieved groan. How could one small animal cause such pandemonium? And if having him create havoc in her house wasn't enough, other people had witnessed it too – the police officer and the man with the poo bags earlier, for instance.

Remembering how the man had looked at her, first with anger and then with incredulity, made her squirm. She couldn't help it if she didn't know the first thing about dogs. She'd never wanted to know and had never had to. The guy needn't have been so snotty about it. And the way he'd jumped to the conclusion that Bertie was hers, irked her somewhat. He could have at least asked first.

She hoped he was more forgiving with the poor dog he'd been carrying. He'd had it tucked under his arm, and it had looked petrified. Gretta didn't blame it. He was a big hulk of a man, tall and muscular, and somewhat unkempt. Good looking, though, if a bit rough around the edges with his shoulder length golden hair and wayward beard.

Bertie whined again, reminding her that she had a living room to tidy up, and she sighed.

She'd only been taking care of the dog for around five hours. It felt like five days.

'SHE'S BACK IN TOWN.' Jakob wasn't talking to himself, he was speaking to the dogs, but his comment earned him a suspicious look from a woman with the smallest chihuahua he'd ever seen.

He wondered whether he should explain, but decided not to bother. He didn't care what others thought of him, even though that had been the problem. Clare had always put a lot of store by appearances and Jakob had never measured up, although he'd tried. God, how he'd tried, but it had never been enough.

Without meeting his eye, the woman sidestepped him, clicking her tongue at her dog (who looked up at Jakob and wagged its tail) and carried on walking. Jakob knew how people viewed him, but he couldn't do anything about his size and the rest of it – his beard and his clothes, for instance – he lacked the inclination to change. He'd tried doing that and it hadn't made an iota of difference: Clare had left anyway. Physically only the once, but emotionally she'd left several times, and each time he'd confronted her about her infidelity she'd promised not to be unfaithful again.

The last time had been the final straw. Forgiving Clare for sleeping with some random bloke was one thing: forgiving her for sleeping with his best mate was another. No wonder Jakob preferred dogs to people. Dogs didn't betray or ridicule. Dogs were loyal and non-judgemental. Dogs accepted people for who they were, faults and all.

A dog's love was unconditional and uncomplicated.

In Jakob's opinion, nothing could compare to the love of a dog. Which was why he was determined to bring Trixie out of her shell and find a loving home for her. The little dog deserved no less.

As he watched Stan and Ripley trotting ahead, tails up and heads down as they sniffed their way along the path, his thoughts flickered to the woman he'd encountered outside the post office.

She'd been clueless. Mind you, she'd claimed that the dog wasn't hers and that she'd been saddled with it. Not for long, he hoped, because the little critter didn't deserve to be in the care of someone who regarded him as a nuisance or a burden. Jakob hoped she treated her cat better.

He snorted: a *scoop* indeed! Then he recalled her face when she thought the Frenchie might poop again on the walk, and he chuckled. She'd looked horrified.

She'd also been very attractive, in an understated way. Not showy like Clare, but more natural. His ex reminded him of an Afghan hound, with her flowing silky hair and haughty expression. But that's where the similarity ended, because Afghans were renowned for their loyalty and Clare hadn't known the meaning of the word.

And there he was again, thinking about her. Why did she have to come back? Was his former best mate with her? The last time Jakob had clapped eyes on her was three years ago, and during those three years, he'd worked hard to forget her.

He'd hoped he was over her. *But was he?*

CHAPTER FOUR

GRETTA WAS A LIGHT sleeper. She hadn't always been that way, but she'd trained herself to wake easily. Whilst her survival hadn't depended on it (Landon had never been violent), her mental health had. As a consequence, she was easily disturbed, and a dog trying repeatedly to jump up on the bed was the epitome of disturbing.

She'd tried the kitchen thing, but before she'd put one foot on the stairs to go to bed, Bertie had started: barking first, then howling. For such a small dog, he could make an impressively big noise. So she'd resorted to taking him upstairs with her, mindful that both she and the neighbours needed their sleep. However, even though Bertie had stopped making a racket, therefore ensuring that any sleeplessness on her neighbor's part wasn't down to *him*, Gretta hadn't slept a wink.

It was now three in the morning and the damn dog had once again jumped on the bed. She was too weary to push him off this time. At least he didn't stink. Having had two baths, he smelt of her favourite shampoo since she'd been forced to use half a bottle on him.

Zaza was nowhere in sight. Gretta didn't expect her to be. The cat slept in her room, but with the dog in residence, she'd buggered off and Gretta felt terrible about that.

This situation clearly couldn't go on. If no one turned up tomorrow (*today* actually, since it was already morning despite Gretta not having gone to sleep yet), she'd contact the kennels that Gio, her police officer neighbour, had mentioned.

There was no way she was putting herself through another night with Bertie under her roof, and she wasn't taking the risk that she might be talked out of her decision, so instead of phoning the kennels beforehand, she decided simply to turn up. If she had to plead with them to take Bertie, then that's what she would do, because there was no way she would bring him back home with her. Not after tonight.

Bertie didn't do himself any favours in the morning either, scoffing Zaza's food when Gretta's back was turned, then cocking his leg against the washing machine. Luckily, Gretta saw what he was about to do and scolded him before he had a chance to water it. Then she immediately felt contrite when she realised she hadn't let him out for a wee yet.

Forced to stand in the garden to keep an eye on him in case he decided to do some more digging, Gretta was frustrated when he took his own sweet time to relieve himself. Her disgust when she had to pick up the smelly dollop he left in the middle of her small square of lawn, knew no bounds.

She used a bag, like the man yesterday did, but still...*Yuck!*

After washing her hands for several minutes in the hottest water she could stand, she hoped she'd never have to do that again.

She was also heartily sick of having a dog permanently attached to her when she went from room to room. He followed her everywhere. She found herself on constant high alert and her stress levels were through the roof. It was almost as bad as when—

No. She refused to think about that. Landon didn't deserve to be thought about. But old habits die hard, and she knew that some of the ones she'd acquired while living with him would probably stay with her for life – her inability to trust again, being one of them.

Stop it, she told herself. Think about something else. *Work,* that was always good for taking her mind off things, and it wasn't as though she didn't have any to be going on with. She had plenty, and there were more clients requiring her services if she wanted to take them on.

However, when Gretta sat at her desk, she found herself unable to settle. And neither could Bertie. Actually, Bertie's restlessness was probably the reason *why* she was unable to focus, since he was padding around her office like a caged animal, and every so often scratching at the door.

She wondered whether he was bored.

Or whether he was pining for his owner. Gretta hoped it was the former. Even though she didn't much care for the little dog, she didn't like to think of him as grieving.

Who was she kidding? Dogs didn't grieve.

Did they?

But whether they did or didn't, this one was going to have to go. *Today.* Because if she didn't get some sleep tonight, she didn't know how she would cope.

JAKOB HEARD A VEHICLE trundling along the road leading to The Forever Home Kennels but ignored it and carried on teaching the Doberman some basic commands. The dog was large for his breed, strong and boisterous. He was two-years old and lacked manners, so no wonder his previous owners (a family with two young children) had been unable to cope with him. Dogs were a commitment and needed love, patience and *training,* all of which took time and effort. Jakob knew that this one would make the right person a wonderful companion.

He hesitated to use the word 'pet.' Dogs weren't like stick insects or goldfish. Dogs needed to be part of the family. 'Companion' was a far more appropriate term.

'Sit,' he commanded.

Rufus sat, his gaze fixed on the treat in Jakob's hand. Foodies were easier to train, and this hound would do anything for a snackeroonie. He was eager to please and intelligent too: a nice combination.

'Good boy,' Jakob said, allowing the dog to hoover the treat off his palm. 'Stay.' He held up a hand and took a step back.

Rufus wriggled impatiently, his back end lifting off the ground.

'No, *stay*.' Jakob's tone was friendly but firm.

Rufus subsided and Jakob took another step back. The dog didn't move, so he risked another. He was pleased that Rufus's eyes were focused on his face, and not on his fingers, which were delving into a pouch at his waist where the treats were kept.

'Jakob? Jakob!' He heard Maisie calling and as he gave the dog the promised morsel, he turned to see her waving.

She had someone with her, and it took him a moment to realise he'd seen her before.

It was the woman from yesterday, the one with the black and white French bulldog.

Jakob called Rufus to heel and clipped the lead onto his harness. The dog surged ahead, eager to greet the newcomers, but Jakob reined him in with a click of his tongue and a quick snap of the leash, enough to get the dog's attention but not too forceful. Rufus, remembering his training, walked to heel, if only briefly. It was a step in the right direction.

'Maisie?' Jakob asked when he was close enough. His attention was drawn to the woman, who looked anxious, and then the dog, who looked distinctly unhappy. The

Frenchie's ears were down, his back hunched. He looked almost as depressed as Trixie, and Jakob wondered what was going on in his little life to make him so despondent.

Maisie said, 'Jakob, this is Gretta Laverne. She's here to surrender her dog.'

'It's not *my* dog,' the woman snapped, then she caught herself. 'Sorry, lack of sleep. He's kept me awake all night.' The strain around her eyes and the dark circles beneath them backed up her claim.

There was also recognition in them, and he knew she remembered him.

Maisie frowned. 'Is he a stray?' Crouching down, she held out her hand. The dog backed away and she straightened up ruefully.

'No, he belongs – *belonged* – to my neighbour. Unfortunately, Mr Butler passed away yesterday, but before he did, he asked me to look after his dog.'

'Yesterday?' Jakob's surprise was reflected in his voice. Was *this* her way of looking after the little fella? At least it explained the poo incident.

'I'm sorry,' she continued. 'I can't keep him. I've got a cat, you see and—'

'So you said.' His interruption was curt.

She scowled. 'I don't want to do this, but I don't have any choice. My cat hates him and it's not fair on her, even if it might only be for a day or so.'

'What do you mean?' Jakob asked.

'I'm hoping a relative will turn up. I've been waiting all day, but...'

'And when they didn't, you thought you'd bring him here?' Jakob was struggling not to let his disgust show, but she picked up on it anyway.

'What would you have me do?' She was shaking her head, and Maisie gave him a warning look.

Even though the animal intake side of things was nothing to do with Maisie, Jakob heeded her advice. 'You're right,' he said. 'But it's only been a day.'

'And a night. Let's not forget the night because, believe me, if I don't get some sleep, I won't be responsible for my actions.'

'He's probably missing his owner, aren't you, boy?' He knelt and held out his hand. 'What's his name?'

'Bertie.'

'Hello, Bertie.' His voice was soft.

The dog stepped forward and sniffed him warily, then retreated to hide behind Gretta's legs. He knew something was afoot.

Was that regret on the woman's face, Jakob wondered, as an expression flickered across it.

'I've spoken to the police,' she said, 'and they told me I should call the dog warden, then if no one came to collect him, he'd be given to an animal shelter for re-homing.'

'So you thought you'd bypass the dog warden?'

She scowled again and addressed her next comment to Maisie. 'Gio – I believe he's your brother-in-law? – suggested I bring him here.'

'Gio did? Oh, okay.' Maisie made a face and said to Jakob, 'We can take him, can't we?'

'I suppose we'll have to.' Jakob glared at Gretta. He didn't see that they had any choice since she was adamant she wasn't going to look after the poor little mite any longer.

'Thank you.' Gretta handed him Bertie's lead. Her tone was pure ice.

Jakob ignored her. 'Come on, boy, let's find you a nice warm kennel.'

He turned to walk away, Bertie on one side of him, Rufus on the other, then hesitated as she asked, 'Will you put him up for adoption straight away?'

'He'll need to have a medical first and be assessed. Then there's the question of his ownership. What if a relative comes looking for him?'

'I've left a note in Mr Butler's house to say he's here. And when someone turns up, I'll point them in your direction. I'm sure it won't be long.'

Jakob didn't share her optimism. He'd seen far too often how easily animals were discarded by relatives of the deceased. 'Come on,' he repeated to the dog. But Bertie was reluctant to go with him, and Jakob could fully understand why. He'd obviously formed an attachment to Gretta, and now his life was about to be turned upside down again.

Bertie hung back, digging his paws in, and whined piteously.

If Jakob hadn't been looking at Gretta at that precise moment, he wouldn't have known that she was moved by what she was doing, but he noticed her eyes grow damp and her chin wobble as she said, 'Bye, Bertie. Be a good boy.'

And then she was gone, leaving Jakob staring after her thoughtfully.

IT WAS RIDICULOUS how awful Gretta felt. Bertie was just a dog. Okay, not *just* a dog, in the same way that Zaza wasn't *just* a cat. He had feelings and had made them known. But Gretta had Zaza to consider, and her cat had to come first. And it wasn't as though Bertie was going to be at The Forever Home for long. Soon, hopefully tomorrow, one of Mr Butler's relatives would turn up at the house, see Gretta's note, and go fetch him. Then she could put this whole thing behind her.

Apart from the funeral, that is. Prior to finding Mr Butler on the floor of his sitting room, it would never have occurred to her to attend his funeral, but now she felt she needed to pay her respects. And if she got the chance, she'd tell him that Bertie was okay.

But Bertie *wasn't* okay, was he? And far from looking after him, Gretta had broken her promise. Poor Mr Butler must have understood he was dying, and his last thoughts had been for his dog.

As she drove along Picklewick's high street, Gretta tried to push her guilt to one side. Viewing the situation from a different perspective, she could honestly say that she *had* looked after Bertie. She'd made sure he was in a place of safety and that he was getting the care he needed. The dog was certainly better off with Jakob than he'd been with *her*. Jakob liked dogs for one thing, and he knew what to do with them and how to take care of them.

And Bertie must surely be happier in a kennel with lots of other dogs around, rather than with her and her cat. In her house he'd been shouted at, locked outside, bathed twice (which he'd loathed) and tied up for much of the time.

Now she'd thought of it like that, Gretta realised she sounded like a monster who hated him and hadn't cared about his welfare; but that wasn't true at all. She *did* care – in as much that she didn't want him to come to any harm. He was in the best place. He *was*.

Gretta told herself that all the way home, and she believed it.

So why did she feel so bad?

Zaza, on the other paw, didn't feel bad at all. The cat took a great deal of persuading to come out from wherever she'd been hiding, and she slunk down the stairs, one wary, distrustful paw at a time. She was clearly still cross and upset, but after a careful and thorough prowl around the house, during which she realised Bertie was no longer in residence, she relaxed. She did that by demanding to be fed, and *hand fed* at that, sitting primly by her bowl with her tail wrapped around her paws and wearing a disdainful expression.

Gretta wondered how long it would take for Zaza to forgive her. An hour? A day? *A week?*

Exhausted after such an emotional and disruptive day, along with zero sleep last night, Gretta made some supper, had a hot bath (trying not to think about Bertie's mournful expression when she'd dumped him in it for the second time in a row yesterday), then retired to bed.

Back to normal tomorrow, she told herself with relief. She disliked even the minimal of disruption, so the past couple of days had been rather trying.

More than trying – they'd been impossible.

But even as she snuggled into her nice calm bed with Zaza purring by her side, Gretta couldn't help feeling guilty. She mightn't have *technically* broken a promise made to a dying man, but she'd broken it *in spirit*.

And now she couldn't get to sleep because she felt so bad.

With a muted scream of frustration, Gretta threw back the covers.

If she couldn't sleep, she may as well do some work.

It was her go-to method of taking her mind off things she didn't want to think about, and she most definitely *didn't* want to think about Bertie's reproachful eyes, or Jakob's disappointed ones.

CHAPTER FIVE

NOT ANOTHER ONE, Jakob thought, as he gazed into Bertie's kennel the following morning.

The dog was in a ball – or as much of a ball as a solid and slightly pudgy Frenchie could curl himself into. His eyes moved when Jakob opened the gate, but not much else.

No dogs belonged in an animal sanctuary, but some coped better in kennels than others. Unfortunately, Bertie wasn't one of them. He'd clearly led a pampered life and had been very much loved, and Jakob would bet his last penny that the little chap had never been in a boarding kennel situation in his life, not even for his owner to go on holiday.

Bertie was shutting down, withdrawing into himself, and Jakob's heart went out to him. He wished he could take him home, but he already had one closed-off dog and she needed as much love and attention as he could give her. Two would be pushing it, especially since he knew that Bertie had been an only dog. Being placed into a home with three others mightn't be good for him.

Jakob would give him a couple of days to see if he settled, and if he didn't he'd ask Dawn if one of the registered foster homes could take him until his owner's relatives could be located.

He wondered how the search was coming along. The hospital would hold on to the deceased for the time being whilst enquiries were made, but Jakob wasn't sure whether it would be the police doing the enquiring or the council. And in the meantime, poor little Bertie was in limbo.

'Come on, fella, let's have a look at you,' Jakob said, kneeling next to the dog's bed.

Bertie didn't stir, so Jakob gently picked him up and stood him on his feet.

Whilst Jakob wasn't medically trained, he was qualified to check an animal's condition to determine whether a trip to the vet was necessary. In this instance, it wasn't. Apart from being on the portly side, which was a tendency of the breed, Bertie appeared to be in good health: clean ears, clear eyes, pink gums, and a shiny coat.

'How about a walk? Walkies?'

No response, apart from a gradual sinking of his haunches as Bertie slowly sat down.

Jakob ruffled his ears, talking to him softly, trying to reassure him. It was a pity Gretta Laverne hadn't felt able to look after him for a few more days. From her expression and the hitch in her voice, she'd felt bad about abandoning him, and Bertie had obviously developed some kind of bond with her, even if it was merely the more familiar versus the totally unknown.

Jakob's phone rang, startling him. It was Dawn.

'Can I patch this call through to you?' she asked. 'It's the woman who surrendered the French bulldog yesterday.'

'Put her through.' He'd filled Dawn in on the new arrival shortly after Gretta had dropped Bertie off and although it was unorthodox, Dawn had agreed with his decision to accept the dog.

'Hi, I'm Gretta Laverne? I brought a dog in yesterday?' Her voice was hesitant and uncertain, the sentences ending on an upward lilt as though she was asking whether he remembered her.

Little did she know that he rarely forgot a dog, although it was unusual for him to remember a person. He remembered *her*, though...

He hoped she had good news for him and that someone had turned up to take the little dog home – wherever that might be.

'Hi,' he replied.

'It's Jakob, right?'

'Yeah.'

'I'm calling because...I just wanted to...'
She stumbled over her words then blurted,
'Is he okay?'

'Not really.' Jakob could tell from her
sharp intake of breath that she'd not been
expecting that. She'd probably been
hoping that he'd say Bertie was fine – but
why should he salve her conscience when
the poor dog was far from fine? Bertie was
miserable and Jakob had no intention of
lying to the woman to make her feel
better.

'Oh, I...what's wrong with him?'

'His owner died and he's been dumped in
a strange place with people he doesn't
know, so you tell me?' As the words left
his lips, Jakob blanched. Dawn wouldn't
be happy with him. She kept trying to instil
in him that he shouldn't be judgemental
with people for giving up their dogs, but

he couldn't help himself. Animals were a commitment and—

Jakob stopped himself right there. Bertie *hadn't* belonged to Gretta. He wasn't *her* dog and never had been. 'Sorry,' he said into the shocked silence. 'I can be blunt sometimes.'

'You don't say.'

He deserved her sarcasm. He'd let his feelings blind him to the fact that this woman didn't have any responsibility towards Bertie. If she couldn't cope with him, she'd done the right thing by bringing him here. And he reminded himself that not everyone loved dogs as much as he did.

'I'm sorry,' he repeated.

'Is he howling a lot?'

'Not at all.'

'Barking?'

'No.'

'What then? Is he off his food?'

'He's beginning to shut down. That's when an animal becomes withdrawn and unresponsive. He's giving up.'

'He can't!'

'He can and he is. It happens sometimes, unfortunately.' His thoughts turned to Trixie: it happened far too often.

'Can anything be done?' Gretta sounded upset, her voice thick with emotion.

'Dawn, the woman you just spoke to at the Thornbury centre, will try to find him a foster home if he doesn't improve over the next few days.'

'What if she can't find one?'

Jakob said, 'Let's hope she can. Or that someone comes to claim him.'

'What if—?' She stopped. 'I'm going to have to come and get him, aren't I?'

'I'm not sure that would be fair to him. He needs stability. You can't be bringing him back again after a day or so.'

'I won't.' She sounded determined, as though she was trying to convince herself.

'But you might.' His tone was gentle.

'He kept crying and chasing my cat. Zaza hates him.'

'Dogs and cats can learn to get on, and he was probably whining because he's pining for his owner.'

'He wasn't whining. Well, he *was*, but I could cope with that because it wasn't all the time. The problem was that whenever I was out of sight, he howled and barked.'

'Sounds like separation anxiety. Was he left on his own much, do you know?'

'I'm not sure, but I don't think so. Mr Butler used to take him everywhere.'

'There's your answer. He's howling because he wants to be with you.'

'But he can't be with me all the time.'

'I understand.' Jakob did, he really did. Velcro dogs (so called because they stuck to their owners the way two pieces of Velcro stuck together) could be challenging, especially for their neighbours, because no one wanted to listen to a noisy dog for hours on end. He added, 'Work, family, kids...I expect you're out of the house a lot.'

'Actually, I'm not. I don't have kids, and I work from home.'

Jakob's ears pricked up. Working from home made having a clingy dog that much easier.

She said, 'But it's the cat, too. They can't be in the same room together.' She sounded upset again.

Jakob had an idea. 'What if I help you introduce your cat to Bertie properly?'

'I don't know. I'm not sure it'll work.'

It had been a long-shot suggestion, he acknowledged silently.

'Do you think it will?' she added.

'It might.'

'What if he still doesn't settle, even if Zara does tolerate him?'

'I'll bring him back to The Forever Home. But before I do that, there are a few tricks we could try which might help.'

'I don't know...' she repeated, but Jakob was on a roll.

'As you said, it might only be for a day or so and just think how much happier he'll be. The poor little scrap has been through such a lot.'

'Is this emotional blackmail?' Her voice was sharp.

'No, it's the truth.'

He heard her sigh. 'I've still got his bowls and his food, and other stuff... I should have brought them with me when I dropped him off, but I didn't think of it.'

Jakob realised he'd lost her. 'Would you like me to pick them up on my way home? I'm sure Bertie would appreciate having familiar things in his kennel.'

'I'm wondering if there was a reason I didn't bring them,' she said.

'Because you thought they might get mixed up with the kennels things and you wanted to give them to his owner's relatives?' he guessed.

'Hmm.' She paused, then said. 'I know I'm going to regret this, but I'm willing to look after him until Mr Butler's next of kin is found. It can't be long, surely? I hate to think of him pining away in a cage.'

It's a nice cage, Jakob wanted to say, but held his tongue.

That was a turn up for the books, he thought after Gretta had given him her address. Although, after seeing her face yesterday when she'd handed the little dog over to him, he hadn't been totally surprised at her change of heart.

Underneath that aloof and exasperated exterior, he suspected Gretta Laverne might be a real softy.

GRETTA WAS KICKING herself. She shouldn't have phoned to see how he was. She should have trusted that the people at The Forever Home Kennels knew what they were doing. Bertie wasn't the first dog they'd have encountered whose owner had passed away.

She should never have let her misplaced guilt get the better of her.

But she knew what it was like to be scared. She knew what it was like to withdraw, to feel like giving up. The difference was that she had been able to extricate herself from her situation. Bertie was powerless to extricate himself from his. He'd have to rely on someone to do that for him. And that someone would have to be her until Mr Butler's relatives were found. She was all Bertie had.

However, Zaza was still Gretta's priority, and if the cat and the dog couldn't resolve their differences, then Bertie really would have to go. And if she had another horrendous night with him, he'd have to go then, too.

Gretta wasn't sure what time Jakob would turn up with Bertie, so she hastily had a quick tidy up (not that it needed doing, but old habits and all that...). The curtain pole was unlikely to be the same again, and one of the ornaments on the bookcase wouldn't recover and had been consigned to the bin, but the sitting room looked presentable enough.

After that, she went to her office and lost herself in work for a few hours.

It was close to four p. m. before she heard the doorbell ring, and she hastened to answer it.

For some reason her stomach did a flippety-flop when she saw Jakob. There was something about him that unsettled her, though not in a nasty way. He had an open, honest face and kind eyes. Actually, they were rather sexy eyes, light blue, ringed with dark lashes and with a crinkling of crow's feet at the corners. He had a pleasant smile too, and she couldn't help smiling back.

Gesturing for him to enter, she stepped aside, and as he brushed past her in the narrow hallway she caught a whiff of citrus and sandalwood. Being this near to him brought it home to her just how big and powerful he was, yet he was carrying Bertie with care, his large hands gentle as he caressed the dog.

Seeing them sent a shiver down her spine as she had a brief image of those hands on her body – would he be as gentle with *her?*

Alarmed at the direction her thoughts had taken, she kept her gaze on the dog as Jakob put him on the floor, and as soon as he was free, Bertie danced on his hind legs, his front paws scrabbling at her as he asked to be petted. He was uttering little whimpers.

'I think someone is pleased to see you,' Jakob said, and Gretta's heart gave a squeeze.

'I think he's just glad to be somewhere he recognises,' she replied. 'He doesn't really know me.'

She noticed that Jakob hadn't relinquished the lead, and she was glad he wasn't taking any chances with her cat.

'He doesn't?' he clarified.

She shook her head. 'I've seen him in the garden and out with Mr Butler, but until the day before yesterday, we'd never met.'

'Where's your cat?'

'She's upstairs.'

'Do you want to go fetch her?'

No, she didn't. Zaza would not take kindly to this. Reluctantly, Gretta climbed the stairs. 'Zaza, come see,' she called.

Zaza, true to her nature, waited for Gretta to come to her.

She was sprawled on Gretta's bed, and when she saw her, she stretched luxuriously, rolling onto her back to show off her fluffy tummy. Gretta wasn't fooled, and resisted the invitation to tickle it because the invitation held sheathed danger. Gretta knew from experience that if she dared tickle her, Zaza's claws would come out and she wasn't scared of using them.

As though sensing something was up, the cat rolled over onto her stomach, her expression inscrutable, but the tip of her tail twitched with low-grade irritation.

Gretta picked her up and steeled herself to carry her downstairs. She had a feeling this wasn't going to be pretty...

It wasn't – but not in the way she'd expected.

Instead of Bertie going ballistic on the end of his lead as he tried to chase Zaza, the dog's ears went down and he crouched on the floor. And Zaza, instead of leaping out of Gretta's arms and doing a mad dash upstairs, lay there, growling. The dog refused to look at the cat, apart from the occasional swift, worried glance.

'How did you do that?' Gretta breathed.

'I didn't do anything. Zaza can see that he's restrained, so she doesn't need to run away, and because she's not running, Bertie's chase instinct isn't activated. Put her down.'

Cautiously, Gretta did as Jakob asked, still worried, even though she knew Bertie couldn't get at her cat.

Zaza sat immobile. Her fur was fluffed up more than usual and she hadn't taken her eyes off the intruder, but she seemed calm enough.

Without making a song and dance about it, Jakob let the lead fall to the floor.

Gretta bit her lip.

'Don't worry,' he said quietly, 'I'll put my foot on it if he misbehaves.'

Bertie stayed put, and for several minutes there was a stand-off, the two animals staring at each other. Then Bertie's impatience got the better of him and he crept forward.

Zaza glowered, and Bertie stopped, looking up at Gretta uncertainly.

'Tell him no,' Jakob instructed.

'No...'

'Sound as though you mean it.'

'No!'

'Perfect.'

Bertie whined.

'Ignore him. He needs to decide for himself what the best course of action is.'

The dog wriggled forward another few centimetres and Zaza's mouth opened in a silent warning and she flashed her canine teeth.

'No,' Gretta told him firmly again, and as Bertie subsided she asked, 'How long do we keep this up?'

'For as long as it takes.'

'It could take hours.'

'It won't.' Jakob sounded confident.

His confidence was spot on she saw, when Bertie, unable to stand the tension, got to his feet.

Zaza's silent hiss became a very vocal one as she spat at him and Bertie took a step back. Zaza hissed again, followed by a throaty growl.

Bertie, his courage deserting him, backed away until he'd put Jakob's legs between him and the cat. Then Zaza calmly got to her feet and with one final snooty look, stalked off with her tail held high.

Bertie looked defeated.

Jakob said, 'I think that's settled. They've sorted out who's boss and it isn't Bertie.'

'You knew that was going to happen, didn't you?'

'I suspected it might.'

'Thank you.'

'You're welcome. I'm sure he'll be fine now, but if you're worried, call me,' he said, and gave her his phone number.

Gretta was amazed and incredibly thankful. She wasn't totally sure she believed what she'd just seen, or that it would last, but that it had happened at all gave her hope she'd made the right decision in having Bertie back.

Unfortunately, she would soon wish she hadn't!

CHAPTER SIX

OKAY, THAT WASN'T SO bad, Gretta thought, when she opened her eyes the next morning. The fact that she'd *woken up* meant she'd had *some* sleep and hadn't lain awake all night arguing with the dog.

A firm 'No' or two from her when Bertie had tried to jump onto the bed seemed to have done the trick. Tonight (if he was still with her by then, and she was hoping he wouldn't be) she would attempt to get him to settle in the kitchen. Having a dog in the bedroom wasn't acceptable, but at least he'd spent the night on the floor where he belonged.

She was lying on her right side, on the side of the bed that used to be hers once upon a time (old habits) and it took her a moment to realise something wasn't right.

It was the smell that alerted her. A distinctly doggy smell...

Slowly, she rolled onto her other side – and came face-to-face with *Bertie*.

He was sprawled across her pillow, fast asleep, and as she glared at him, his paws twitched and he uttered little huffing breaths. He was dreaming.

If she hadn't been so appalled that he'd spent the night in her bed, she might have thought it cute.

Where was Zaza? Her cat normally slept with her. If he'd ousted her, Gretta would be most displeased.

But to her surprise, Zaza was lying at the foot of the bed.

Gretta had taken a risk in allowing both animals access to the bedroom, but after Jakob's intervention yesterday, cat and dog had appeared to get along. Actually, that wasn't the right turn of phrase: Zaza had ignored Bertie with calculated contempt, apart from when he got too close and then she'd hissed and spagged him. It had taken one swipe of a clawed paw across his nose, which had made him yelp, for Bertie to be put in his place.

All evening, he'd kept shooting Zaza anxious and slightly pleading looks, as though he wanted to make friends but didn't dare, and slowly Gretta had relaxed, although she'd continued to keep a very wary eye on the dog, until she was convinced that Zaza had the upper hand and Bertie respected the cat's boundaries.

Which was why Gretta was surprised to find both animals on her bed this morning. But not pleased. She was far from pleased.

Now she'd have to wash the bedding, and when a suspicious noise came from Bertie's back end, followed by a fug of revolting smell, she let out a cry of disgust and leapt out of bed.

Bertie woke with a startled grunt, saw her and wagged his tiny tail, a worried expression in his eyes. Gretta immediately felt awful; he thought he was about to get a telling off, which he should do considering she'd made it plain that he wasn't welcome on the bed and he knew he was in the wrong; but she couldn't bring herself to scold him.

Who knew that dogs' faces could be so full of expression?

'Off,' she told him, and he got to his feet and slunk to the edge of the bed, dropping onto the floor with a thud. Zaza watched him, and Gretta wondered what the cat was thinking.

It was early, about six thirty, but that was a good thing, because she wanted to get stuck into a new project that one of her clients had tasked her with. Re-vamping a website was right up her street and would keep her busy for hours.

She supposed she should take Bertie for a walk at some point. She'd read that a tired dog was a happy dog, and surely those little legs of his wouldn't take a lot of walking to wear them out?

A shower first though, then breakfast.

To her consternation, Bertie followed her into the bathroom and sat watching as she began to remove her pyjamas. Thinking that he might need a wee, she ushered him downstairs, and this time she wasn't moved by his hurt expression as she shoved him into the garden and closed the door on his flat little face. He could stay there until she'd finished showering, as there was no way she was going to do that with an audience!

'I CAN'T FIND HIM! He's disappeared!' Gretta's voice was panicked.

'Whoa, slow down. What do you mean you can't find him?' When Jakob thought he might hear from Gretta again, he'd assumed it would be because she couldn't cope with the Frenchie, not because she'd *lost* him.

'I let him into the garden for a wee and when I went to let him back in, he wasn't there. I've been calling and calling.' She hitched in a breath. 'It's my fault. I should have let him stay in the bathroom with me, but I didn't want him watching me take a shower.'

Jakob's own breath caught as an image of Gretta naked, with water cascading over her, swam into his head.

Shocked, he blinked to clear it, as she continued, 'I can't see how he could have got out. There's a six-foot fence all around.' She wailed, 'I don't know what to do.'

'I'll come right over.' It was his day off and he hadn't intended to go anywhere near Picklewick today, but needs must. He'd have to take the dogs with him though, as he didn't know how long he'd be out.

Jakob had a quick shower of his own, trying not to think about Gretta as he did so, grabbed a couple of brownies in lieu of a proper breakfast, and bundled the dogs into the car.

His two bounded into their crates, full of enthusiasm (they loved a car ride), but Trixie was more reluctant, so Jakob lifted her up and gently deposited her in the same crate as Ripley. Ripley, bless him, gave her a reassuring lick on the nose.

She was still nervous and anxious, but Jakob could see that she was taking her cues from his dogs, trusting them before she'd learn to trust him, but he was okay with that. She'd get there eventually and when she did, she'd be ready for her forever home.

Gretta was peering through the window when Jakob pulled up in front of her house and she hurried to open the door.

She looked so worried that his heart gave a squeeze and he had an urge to take her in his arms and comfort her, but he hastily squashed it. He was done with holding women, because holding didn't mean *keeping hold*. He'd failed spectacularly in keeping hold of Clare. She'd repeatedly slipped through his fingers until one day she'd been gone for good.

Concerned that Clare was continuing to invade his thoughts, Jakob's voice was gruffer than he intended when he said to Gretta, 'Show me.'

Wordlessly, she led him through the kitchen and into the garden.

It was oblong, around ten metres long and as wide as the house, so not too big. It sported a square lawn surrounded by shrubs and bushes, with a terrace leading off the back door. In the corner was a wooden shed, and the whole thing was enclosed by a high burlap fence. Jakob would be shocked if the dog had scaled it, although it wasn't unheard of for small dogs to get over high fences. Bertie, however, was too portly for such athleticism. He might get *through* it though, and with that in mind, Jakob peered under the bushes and behind the shrubs.

'He's not hiding,' Gretta said. 'I checked.'

'Ah, but did you check for gaps in the fence?'

'There aren't any.'

He paused, holding aside a dense shrub. 'There *wasn't*,' he corrected. 'But there is now.'

The hole was small and unobtrusive, and it wasn't in the fence itself. Bertie had dug underneath it.

'The little…' Gretta trailed off. 'So *that's* what he was doing the other day when he was covered in dirt. He must have been digging.'

'Is that Mr Butler's house?' Jakob guessed, and she nodded.

'Why isn't he coming back when I call him?' she asked. 'He can't get in the house, so he must be in the garden.'

'Because he doesn't want to. He's looking for his owner.'

'Oh, that's so sad.'

'It is, isn't it?' Jakob agreed, gazing over the fence, his height giving him an advantage. 'I see him.'

'What's he doing?'

'Sitting on the step.'

Bertie looked thoroughly despondent, and Jakob's heart melted. Animals didn't understand when their owners died, and it was awful to see their continual hope that their human would appear.

Jakob asked, 'This might sound awful, but was Mr Butler still alive the last time Bertie saw him?'

'Yes. They took him away in an ambulance.'

'That explains it. Bertie is expecting him to come back.'

Gretta's eyes filled with tears, and once again he wanted to comfort her. 'Let's go get him,' he said instead.

'He'll do it again, won't he?'

'Probably.'

'How can I stop him? I mean, I can block up this hole, but he'll only dig another.'

'That's his home, so it's only natural he wants to go back to it. It's a pity you don't have anything of Mr Butler's with his scent on. It might help comfort him.'

'I could get something,' she said. 'I've still got a key to his house. Would you come with me?'

'As long as we're quick. I've got my own dogs in the car. I was about to take them for a walk when you phoned.'

'I haven't taken Bertie out yet,' she said.

Was she hinting that he could walk Bertie for her? Because if so, it was a bit of a cheek. She'd already disrupted his morning.

As she fetched the key to next door, she said, 'I'm not sure where to take him.'

'Around the block will do. But don't let him off the lead,' he warned.

'I wasn't planning on it. Isn't there anywhere more exciting than around the block?'

'You tell me – you're the one who lives in Picklewick.'

'I hardly know the area. My walks are to the shops and back.'

'You're not local?' He was surprised.

'No.' She stepped into the street, looked up and down it, then locked her front door. Blimey, Jakob thought, how long did she expect to be in her neighbour's house for?

'Habit,' she explained, when she saw him staring. 'Can't be too careful.'

Despite Mr Butler having only been gone a couple of days, the place already felt unlived in, and Jakob wondered whether

Bertie sensed it too, because as soon as the dog trotted inside, his expression hopeful, he stopped and his whole demeanour changed. Jakob's heart went out to him as he dashed from room to room, whining, his cries becoming more heart-wrenching as he realised his owner wasn't there.

Gretta shot Jakob a desperate look. 'There must be *something* we can do.'

'Unfortunately, there isn't.'

'I hope someone comes to fetch him soon.'

So did Jakob. The sooner little Bertie was settled, the better.

'What should I take?' Gretta asked, gazing around.

'Something with his owner's scent on: a scarf, a shirt...anything as long as it hasn't been laundered recently.'

'Will this do?' She held up a bobbled navy cardigan.

Jakob took it from her and offered it to Bertie to sniff. The dog whined again. 'I think so,' he said, and was relieved when Gretta picked Bertie up and carried him to the front door. The dog's sadness was palpable.

'If that's all—' he began, eager to see to his own precious pooches, but Gretta cut him off.

'Can I come with you?'

Jakob hesitated, a suspicion beginning to form. 'You've never taken a dog for a walk before, have you?' He didn't think the trip to the Post Office counted.

'So? I bet you've never formatted an ebook before.'

'Is that what you do?'

'One of the things.' She gazed at him defiantly.

'You're right, I'm sorry. Not everyone likes dogs.'

'It's not that I don't like them...'

'But you're more of a cat person?'

'Correct. So, can I come with you on your walk?'

'It'll be a long one,' he warned.

'That's fine. I don't mind a long walk, but could I grab some breakfast first? I can make you something, too?'

'I've got my dogs with me,' he reminded her. 'I don't like leaving them in the car for long. How about we grab a coffee and something to go from the cafe in the village? I haven't had any breakfast yet, either. I was going to have a brownie.'

Gretta stopped, a hand to her mouth. 'Oh, God, I'm sorry. I was in such a panic, I didn't think. You've got to get to work and—'

'It's my day off.'

'In that case, I'm sure you've got more important things to do than spend it running around after a dimwit woman who is nervous about taking a dog for a walk.'

Actually, he didn't, and the thought of spending time with Gretta was rather appealing.

However, he brushed that aside and convinced himself the real reason was that he wanted to make sure she knew how to take care of Bertie if no one came forward. And that maybe, *just maybe*, if no one claimed him, Bertie might find his forever home with Gretta.

Jakob even managed to make himself believe it – because what other reason could there be since he'd vowed to never again risk losing his heart?

CHAPTER SEVEN

GRETTA WAS AMAZED how well Jakob could control three dogs on leads when she had her hands full with just the one. Bertie seemed to be over-excited at being out and kept trotting around her, forcing her to swap the lead from one hand to the other. And when he wasn't doing that, he was lunging and pulling, or yanking at her arm when he stopped suddenly to sniff at something.

Jakob's dogs were all walking nicely, although the scruffy one by the name of Trixie seemed to be more timid than well-trained.

'I'm fostering her for the time being,' Jakob explained when Gretta mentioned that she seemed a little scared. 'We've no idea of her history, but I suspect she might have been abused.'

Gretta's heart constricted. She mightn't be a dog lover, but she simply couldn't imagine how anyone could hurt one. 'How long will you foster her for?'

'For as long as it takes. If we can't find a forever home for her, I'd like to get her to a point where she can go back to the kennels to live.'

'You wouldn't keep her?'

'I can't keep them all,' he replied sadly. 'There are so many dogs who need our help. Another one will soon come along who finds kennel life hard.'

'Like Bertie?'

'Exactly like Bertie. Do you want me to hold him while you order some food?'

They'd arrived at the cafe, and by mutual agreement they'd decided to eat there, rather than grab something to take with them. There were a couple of tables outside, and since the weather was nice, they could enjoy their breakfast in relative comfort.

'I'll have a bacon sarnie,' he said, fishing in a pocket and withdrawing a wallet.

'*I'm* getting these. I owe you for—'

'You don't owe me anything. I did it for Bertie's benefit.'

'I see.' She pressed her lips together.

Jakob, she was discovering, had little in the way of social graces. He said what he meant. Actually, she decided, as she went inside to place their order, that was a

143

good thing. She'd been subjected to enough mind games with Landon. Jacob saying it as he saw it, was refreshing. And rare. At least she knew where she stood, and she appreciated that more than he would ever know.

She was rapidly coming to the conclusion that he was very much like a dog himself: no subterfuge, no hidden agenda, and he didn't appear to be good at hiding his feelings. Jakob's face and body language were as expressive as Bertie's.

The comparison made her chuckle as she looked through the window and saw him with a pensive look on his face.

When she returned to the table bearing a little treat for each of the four dogs, the first thing he said to her was, 'Have you got any poo bags?'

So *that's* what he'd been thinking about whilst she'd been in the cafe – and she burst out laughing. Then stopped, her eyes wide. When was the last time she'd laughed spontaneously like that? She couldn't remember; it had been such a long time ago. Abruptly, she worried he would take offence, and she shot him a cautious look.

He didn't seem in the least bit bothered that she'd laughed at him. Well, not *at* him, exactly: more *because* of him.

'I don't actually own any,' she admitted, giving Bertie his biscuit. He took it from her delicately and crunched it, scattering crumbs everywhere.

'Here.' Jakob pulled a handful out of his pocket.

She accepted them gingerly and pulled a face.

'They haven't been used,' he assured her.

'Thank goodness for that!' She didn't think they had been. It was just the thought of what was going to go in them that made her feel queasy.

'They're biodegradable, if that's what you're worried about,' he said.

She hadn't even thought about that, but it was nice to know he was concerned about the environment. She shoved the bags in her jean's pocket. 'Thanks. How much do I owe you?'

He gave her a look that she guessed meant he didn't want any money for them.

Over their impromptu breakfast, Gretta realised she wanted to know more about him. It surprised her. She'd been so insular (by her own choice) during these past two years that she believed she didn't need any social interaction, but she discovered she was rather enjoying being in his company.

Might it be because he didn't see her as anything other than someone with a dog? That it was Bertie he was interested in, not her? That if it wasn't for the dog, Jakob wouldn't look at her twice.

To be honest, he wasn't looking at her twice now, or even once. Bertie was what he was interested in, and his attention was currently on the dog, who was lying next to Trixie and licking her ear. Trixie didn't seem to mind.

'How long have you been a...?' Gretta wasn't entirely sure what his job was.

'Kennel supervisor?'

She nodded.

'Five years, give or take.'

'Have you always wanted to work with animals?'

'Always. I can't imagine doing anything else. I'm not good at doing anything else.'

'How do you know?' Her tone was light, almost teasing, which was most unlike her. 'How many jobs have you tried and failed at?'

She was joking, but he took her seriously. 'Too many.'

'Like what?'

'I don't read ebooks.'

'Pardon?'

'You said you format ebooks. At least, I *think* that's what you said.'

As a change of subject, it was clunky and obvious, but Gretta respected his privacy.

After all, she was pretty protective of hers. 'I do, among other things.'

'Like what?'

She smiled as he batted her question back at her. 'I'm a virtual PA, for authors mostly,' and she explained what she did.

She went into more detail than she'd gone into with anyone else, including her family. Not their fault. Hers. She feared that if she told them too much about her life, they'd guess an awful lot more, and she'd hate it if they knew what a mess she'd made of things, how she'd allowed Landon to control her to the extent where she'd almost lost herself. Then there was also the suspicion that they wouldn't be interested anyway. They never had in the past. Gretta had been the invisible child, the quiet sibling. The one no one took much notice of.

'Did you always want to be a virtual PA?' he asked, and for a moment she nearly told him the truth – that she'd ended up being one because Landon had hated her going out to work. He'd wanted her at home, where he could keep an eye on her. Then, after she'd left him, working from home on her own terms and hiding away from the world was what she'd needed. The isolation suited her. After all, during her time with Landon, she'd become very used to it. But the operative phrase here was *on her own terms*. These days she *chose* to live this way: it hadn't been thrust upon her.

'Not always. I kind of fell into it,' she said.

'Do you enjoy it?'

'I wouldn't do it if I didn't.' Her reply was sharp. Never again would she be coerced into doing something she didn't want to do.

'Are you good at it?'

'Very.'

'You don't like people much, either,' he said, and Gretta blinked.

'I like people fine,' she countered steadily.

'*I* don't.' There was that candour again, as though he didn't care what anyone thought. 'I prefer dogs,' he added.

Gretta's lips twitched. 'I prefer cats.'

'We should hate each other.' Jakob grinned at her.

'Who says we don't?' She grinned back, once again thinking how attractive he looked when he smiled. Quite sexy actually, in a rugged kind of way.

'It's marvellous the way a dog can break the ice,' he said. 'Shall we make a move? I think Bertie's getting restless.'

Gretta noticed that Jakob's dogs were still lying patiently, although Trixie looked more worried than patient, whereas Bertie was busily chewing his lead. If she wasn't careful, he was going to chew right through it.

With a shake of her head, she held up the gnawed bit for Jakob to see.

'On the way back, we can pop into the pet shop and buy him a chew,' Jakob suggested. 'It'll keep him quiet and give him an outlet if he's feeling stressed.'

'A chew. Right. Anything else I need to know?'

'Lots,' he replied cheerfully.

Gretta sighed. 'I thought there might be.' But if she was honest, the prospect wasn't as daunting as it could be, especially now that she had an expert on hand to advise her.

'I DIDN'T REALISE there was a path leading from the village to the top of the mountain,' Gretta puffed. They'd left Picklewick behind and were gradually climbing towards what Jakob had informed her was a riding school.

'I don't come this way myself very often,' he said. 'But some of the more active dogs need longer walks.'

Gretta stopped for a breather and looked back the way they'd come. The only time she'd been up here was when she'd taken Bertie to the kennels, and she'd been too tired and too despondent to take much notice of her surroundings.

They'd climbed a fair distance already, she noticed. Picklewick lay in the bottom of a wide river valley, with mountains on both sides. Not high mountains, like the Alps, but high enough for her aching thighs.

Pretending to study the view (in reality she wanted to give her racing heart an opportunity to slow down), she was delighted to see the village spread out below, nestled in the patchwork of fields, meadows and patches of woodland. She tried to make out her house, but because of the angle it was impossible; however, she could see the square turret of the Norman church.

Breathing deeply, the crisp clean air filling her lungs, she let the peace wash over her.

All she could hear was her own heartbeat, the call of a bird overhead, and the wind winnowing through the grass.

Then Bertie tugged on her arm, keen to get going, spoiling the moment, so she let him pull her up the slope.

'We won't go all the way to the top,' Jakob said. 'I don't want Trixie, or Bertie for that matter, to think we're taking them back to The Forever Home.'

'They won't think that, will they?'

'They might. Dogs have an acute sense of smell.'

Gretta sniffed. 'All I can smell is a stinky farmyard.'

'That'll be the horses at the stables,' he laughed. 'You're not much of an outdoorsy person, are you?'

'Not much. I'm assuming you are?'

He shrugged. 'I have to be. Dogs need exercise, and I look after a lot of dogs.'

'Not all by yourself, surely?'

'We have some staff, but not nearly enough, so we rely heavily on volunteers. Since you're kind of fostering Bertie, I suppose *you* could be called a volunteer.'

Gretta rather liked the sound of that; it seemed a worthwhile thing to do, and now that Zaza and Bertie had reached a truce, Gretta didn't feel as stressed. She wouldn't want to do it forever, though. A few days was enough.

'How long should I give it?' she asked abruptly.

'At least seven days. Bertie can't be re-homed until then.'

'It's been four already.'

'Would anyone in the village know whether Mr Butler had any family?'

'When you saw me the other day, I'd just asked at the post office, but they weren't sure. He used to keep himself to himself, apparently. His wife died several years ago, and they didn't have any children.'

'No wonder you looked frazzled.'

'I was a bit. I'd only just found out that he'd died. And Bertie had been making an awful racket. He's made it clear he doesn't like being left on his own.'

'We'll have to do something about that,' Jakob said.

'Like what?'

'You start off small, then build up to longer and longer periods of time.' Jakob must have seen her doubtful expression because he continued, 'I can help with that, if you like?'

'Yes, please, if it's not too much trouble.'

'Nothing is too much trouble when it comes to an animal's welfare,' he replied.

They'd arrived at the stables but didn't linger, the path taking them past a row of three pretty holiday cottages, then up a narrow track and onto Muddypuddle Lane. Gretta recognised it from her journey the other day. There was a farm further up, if she remembered correctly.

'We'll take this track here,' Jakob said when they reached a gate leading to the path onto the hillside. 'Unless you've had enough?'

'I can manage a bit further,' she replied, 'but I don't want to be out too long, as I've got work to do.'

'Fair enough. Another half an hour, then we'll turn back. It'll be easier going downhill.'

Thank heaven for that! Nevertheless, she was glad she'd come. Jakob, despite his sometimes surly manner, was actually quite a nice guy.

But the best bit about being in his company was that he didn't make any demands on her. Even so, it didn't matter whether or not she thought he was nice, or whether or not she found him attractive, because she wasn't going to allow him, or any other man, into her life. Once bitten, twice shy. And Gretta hadn't just been bitten, *she'd had her heart torn out.*

CHAPTER EIGHT

THAT'S WHAT BERTIE had needed, Gretta realised, when she'd been able to work uninterrupted for three hours yesterday after they'd returned from their long walk. It had worn him out. She'd felt a little tired herself, but in a good way. She'd also realised just how unfit she'd become. Maybe having Bertie for a while would be good for her, as it would get her out of the house twice a day, and into the fresh air. It cut into her work time, but surprisingly, she discovered she'd been more productive than usual, as though the unaccustomed exercise had energised her.

And Bertie had slept better last night, which meant she'd slept better too.

Gretta chuckled wryly. She was referring to the dog like she would a baby. Better night's sleep indeed! Once again, he'd spent it on her bed, and once again she'd woken up with his snuffly little face far too close to hers for comfort (*her* comfort: *he'd* been perfectly happy). And she'd been forced to change the sheets yet again, but the situation would hopefully improve tonight as she was praying someone would claim him today. He was quite a sweet little creature and needed to be with someone who could love him the way he deserved to be loved.

After a quick walk to do the necessary this morning, Bertie settled down at her feet as she sat at her computer. She still couldn't move without him shadowing her, which she continued to find disconcerting (a dog pawing at the bathroom door and whining to be let in was rather bothersome). If he stayed with her much longer, his separation anxiety would have to be addressed – and *soon*, because she needed to go shopping. She supposed she could do her weekly shop online, but damn it, she refused to be confined to the house because of a dog.

Her thoughts turned to Jakob and his promise of help. He was due to pop in after work today, but she honestly couldn't wait until then to buy groceries because she was almost out of milk and bread. The corner shop was an option, but wherever she did her shopping Bertie was going to be left on his own for a while, so she may as well go to the supermarket in Thornbury and do what needed to be done. Bite the bullet, so to speak, because Jakob had warned her that curing a dog of separation anxiety wouldn't be quick. In fact, he'd said that it wasn't a cure but should be thought of in terms of managing it. But if Gretta wanted to eat, she couldn't possibly wait until Bertie's separation anxiety was *manageable.*

Not fully trusting the dog to behave himself while she was out (okay, not trusting him *at all*, since he didn't have a very good track record so far when left unsupervised) she decided to take him next door and leave him in his own house for the duration. It was familiar, and a few more scratches on the kitchen door's paintwork wouldn't matter.

So that's what she did; although during the short drive to Thornbury, Bertie's disbelieving and reproachful expression played on her mind. To say he was unhappy at being left alone was an understatement.

Mindful that he was probably howling his little head off at this very minute, Gretta didn't hang about. However, the supermarket was busy and after she'd whizzed up and down the aisles, praying she hadn't forgotten anything essential, she was forced to queue to pay.

Irritably, she tapped her foot, continually scanning the checkouts for the next available free one.

Two women were in front of her and seemed to be having a serious conversation, and when she heard one of them mention the name Jake, Gretta's ears pricked up. They weren't talking about the Jakob she knew, but it had caught her attention, and now that it had she couldn't help listening.

'Your problem is that you always think the grass is greener, when it really isn't,' a woman with a sharp bob said to her companion, who was around Gretta's age. She had long hair caught up in a high ponytail and was wearing a considerable amount of make-up for a trip to the supermarket,

She replied, 'I know. I found that out. But Jake was always so intense, and I wanted some *fun*.'

'That's because he thought the world of you, Clare. He used to worship the ground you walked on.'

'I know,' Clare, the one with the ponytail, repeated with a sigh. 'I think that was the problem.'

The first woman was shaking her head. 'I wish Perry looked at me the way Jake used to look at you. He adored you.'

'Alright, Kelly, no need to rub it in.' Clare's tone was sharp. 'And there's no need to keep harping on about how badly I treated him either, because I know that too. I was a cow to him.'

Kelly snorted. 'And the rest. Did you really think he'd forgive you for sleeping with Byron? You pushed him too far. Have you seen him yet?' Clare shook her head and Kelly asked, 'How do you think he'll react?'

'I honestly don't know. I've been so stupid, Kel. If I could turn the clock back, I would. I'll never find a man who loved me like Jake did. I—'

'There's a till free.' Kelly interrupted her and pushed her overflowing trolley towards it, leaving Clare with her half empty one, biting her lip, and Gretta with half a story and the suspicion that the woman hadn't known how lucky she'd been.

Not all men thought the world of their wives or girlfriends. Not all men worshipped the ground they walked on. If Landon had loved her the way this unknown Jake had loved Clare, things might have been very different indeed.

Feeling melancholy, she paid for her groceries and headed home to the only man in her life now: a small black and white dog – who was only with her because he had nowhere else to go.

JAKOB DIDN'T WORK a traditional nine to five, Monday to Friday, and today he was on a split shift because someone had phoned in sick this morning, which had scuppered his plans for the day.

He'd started work at The Forever Home early, at around six-thirty, but his day had begun even earlier than that since he had his own dogs to see to beforehand. After a brisk walk along the canal as the sun was rising, he'd left the dogs at home tucking into their breakfasts, happy in the knowledge that his dad would pop around later to pick them up and take them to his house for a while, so they wouldn't be left alone for long.

Jakob didn't know how he'd manage if it wasn't for his parents. They were always happy to help and never made a fuss when two dogs became three overnight, which had happened several times over the past few years.

But due to the sickness of a member of staff and him having to now do a split shift, Jakob was currently on his way to their house. He had a couple of hours spare before he had to go back to work, so he thought he'd take the dogs out again to save his parents having to.

Even though he'd phoned ahead to let them know he was coming, his dad had his walking boots and coat on, and three leads in his hand.

After greeting two ecstatic dogs and a more cautious and reserved one (Jakob was pleased to see Trixie give a tentative wag of her tail), Jakob said, 'No need for you to take them out, Dad. I'll do it.'

His mother bustled out from the kitchen and Jakob gave her a hug. Dad had retired a couple of years ago, but Mum still worked part-time. Soon, she would give up work completely and Jakob would have to reconsider his dog sitter options. He didn't want to restrict his parents' ability to go out and about whenever they wanted. They were *his* dogs and it was down to him to make sure their needs were met.

'Do you mind if I come with you?' his dad asked. 'I could do with stretching my legs.'

Jakob caught his mum and dad exchanging a look and he wondered what was going on.

He quickly found out, because no sooner had his father got Jakob on his own than he said, 'Your mum bumped into Clare yesterday. She was coming out of the hairdressers. Clare, not your mother.' He looked uncomfortable, as though he'd drawn the short straw. And maybe he had.

Jakob said nothing, but he could feel the tension as his shoulders hunched and his jaw clenched. He didn't want to have this conversation.

But it looked like he was going to, as his dad ploughed on, 'Your mother's worried about you.'

'She needn't be.'

'Byron isn't with her. Clare is on her own.'

After Clare had slept with his best friend (*ex* best friend, now) and Jakob had found out, the pair of them had left Thornbury for pastures unknown. Rather, *Jakob* hadn't known where they'd gone, and he hadn't wanted to. He'd just been glad that he wouldn't have the worry of bumping into them every time he left the house.

Looking back, he should have realised she was a *bad 'un* as his dad called her, because neither Stan nor Ripley had taken to her. Clare had mostly ignored his dogs, and they had ignored her.

Jakob was realistic enough to understand that just because a dog liked someone, it didn't mean that they were a nice person. But if a dog wasn't keen, then Jakob took notice.

More fool him for being so in love that he'd forgotten that. Or ignored it. Either way, it had bitten him on the backside and had caused him so much heartache.

'Are you okay, Jakob?' His father was gazing at him with concern.

'I'm fine.'

Fortunately, his dad must have felt that he'd done his bit in administering fatherly concern, because the conversation swiftly moved on to Trixie and how she was settling in.

'She's a real sweetheart,' Dad said. 'Your mother is quite taken with her.' He shot Jakob a look, adding hurriedly, 'Don't be getting any ideas. We love borrowing yours now and again, but I wouldn't want a dog full time. Although, I have to admit that they're good company when your mum's at work, and I get a nice bit of exercise when I'm out and about with them. And loads of other dog walkers stop and have a chat.'

'They do,' Jakob agreed, although he wasn't one for stopping and chatting. It was stopping and chatting that had got him into trouble in the first place.

Ripley had been a puppy, and Jakob had been walking home from the vets, the dog tucked into his coat. Ripley had just had a check-up because he had a wonky back leg, which was why he'd been surrendered to the shelter. The breeder knew he was unlikely to sell the dog and had just wanted to get shot of him.

Jakob had fallen in love with the pup, and on the way home from the vet, he'd fallen in love again. This time with a woman. She'd gone all gooey and cooey over the dog, and Jakob, blissfully unaware of what he was letting himself in for, had stopped and chatted.

And he'd regretted doing so every day since he'd found out Clare wasn't a one-man kind of woman.

But he'd loved her, damn it! And now, thanks to his concerned parents, she was in his head once again.

Thankfully, by the time he'd driven to Gretta's house on his way back to work, he'd managed to put Clare out of his head, because he was too busy thinking about Bertie.

He hoped the dog hadn't given Gretta the run around last night, and that he and the cat were still getting along. Zaza, like most cats, was an ace at disdain and could win an Oscar in aloofness, but she was stunning to look at, with her emerald eyes and smoke-grey fur.

Jakob, for all his insistence that he was a dog person and not a cat person, quite liked cats. He respected their air of independence and the way they only accepted affection on their terms. He wished he had been more cat. If he hadn't been so loyal and devoted, and not to mention adoring and forgiving, Clare mightn't have treated him so abysmally.

Stop bloody thinking about her, he scolded himself silently as he rang Gretta's doorbell.

While he waited for her to answer, he self-consciously ran his fingers through his too-long, scruffy hair. His lack of attention to how he looked had been one of Clare's bugbears. She'd forever been nagging him to smarten up, and he'd tried his utmost to be what she'd wanted him to be, but it had never been enough.

Gretta opened the door, a beaming smile on her face. 'Hi.'

'Hello,' he replied, shuffling nervously from foot to foot, relaxing slightly when he spied Bertie at her feet.

The dog scuttled up to him, his behind waggling from side to side. Bertie being so pleased to see him, made him smile.

'Has he been behaving himself?' Jakob asked, his gaze on the dog.

The brief glance he'd taken at Gretta had reminded him how pretty she was. But not in an obvious way. Hers was a more natural look, and he preferred it. Clare used to spend an inordinate amount of time in front of the mirror, preening and applying goodness knows what to her face—

And why the hell was he thinking about her *again?!* Especially since he'd missed Gretta's reply.

'Pardon, I didn't catch that?' he said.

Gretta laughed, and Jakob risked another look. She was shaking her head ruefully.

'He hasn't been behaving himself at all.' Bending down to do some ear ruffling, she said, 'Come in and I'll tell you all about what Bertie has been getting up to.'

She ushered him inside, and he noticed her checking the street, a quick glance up and down it, as though she was expecting someone. Jakob wondered who it might be.

Despite having spent around three hours in her company yesterday, he realised he didn't know anything about her. They'd not spoken about anything personal, which had suited him just fine, but he found himself becoming curious about her.

After closing the door, Gretta led him and Bertie (who was still dancing around his legs and begging for attention) into the sitting room.

'Would you like a drink?' she asked. 'I'm having one. I've been to the supermarket and haven't long got back. By the time I fetched Howl-a-Lot from Mr Butler's house and put the groceries away, it was nearly time for you to call, so I thought I'd wait and have one with you. Do you prefer tea or coffee?'

'Coffee, please.'

She disappeared into the kitchen, and Jakob crouched down to pet Bertie. Bertie, delighted at the turn of events, stood on his back legs and placed his front ones on Jakob's knee. His tongue lolled out as Jakob scratched his ears.

Drinks made, Gretta told him that Bertie had howled and barked from the second she'd left him to the second she'd returned, and the reason she knew this was because her neighbour, Harriet, had been desperate to tell her all about the hideous noise.

'I must admit it was rather loud. I could hear him from the street, and he was shut in the kitchen, which is at the back of the house,' she added.

Jakob said, 'Hopefully I'll be able to help with that, but it won't be a quick fix.'

Her face fell, and he guessed she'd been hoping for a result today. Then she brightened. 'Never mind, he mightn't be here tomorrow.'

Inexplicably, Jakob's heart sank. 'You can't wait to get rid of him, can you?'

Surprise flitted across her face. 'He doesn't belong to me. He belongs to whoever has inherited Mr Butler's estate, unless he's made a different provision for him in his will.'

That was true enough, Jakob thought, hoping that Bertie's new owner would be found soon because the little chap deserved some stability. But until then, Gretta had stepped up to the mark – which was good of her. He must remember that. And Bertie was obviously settling in well.

'Shall we get started?' he suggested, taking a last gulp of the hot coffee. He got to his feet and pulled his car keys out of his pocket.

'Where are you going?' she asked with a frown.

'To fetch a crate from the car. He won't be able to do any damage if he's in there.'

When he brought it in, Bertie trotted over to it, sniffing curiously.

'He probably remembers it, and it might still have his scent. Can you put Mr Butler's cardigan on the bottom for him to lie on? Hopefully, it'll help keep him calm.'

Gretta did as he asked, folding the cardigan and placing it neatly inside.

He said, 'Okay, you're going to put a treat in it and try to persuade him to go in.' He passed her a handful of doggy treats. 'We need to get him used to the crate before we shut him in it. He needs to see that it's non-threatening, just part of the furniture. If he shows any interest in it, I want you to reward him. And if you give him a treat, put it in there, so he has to go inside to get it. When he does, give him lots of praise.'

'Then what? What do we do next?'

'Nothing today.'

'Nothing?'

'I told you it wouldn't be a quick fix. Give it a day or so, then you can start closing the door. Just for a second or two, with you in the room. And preferably after a good long walk, when he's tired and ready for a nap.'

'Oh, okay.'

'I'll leave the crate with you.'

'Don't you need it for your dogs?'

'I'll borrow one from work.'

'Thanks for this. And for the advice. I'll let you get off home.'

'I'm not going home. I'm going back to the kennels. There are the evening feeds to do and a final round of walks.' To his embarrassment, his stomach rumbled loudly. It must have been the mention of food, and he realised that he'd skipped lunch. He'd pick something up from the cafe in Picklewick on the way, assuming it was still open. 'You don't happen to know what time the cafe closes, do you?' he asked, thinking that if it was closed, he'd grab a snack from the convenience store instead.

'Sorry, I don't, but I can make you another coffee before you go, save you buying one.'

His stomach gurgled again, and he winced.

'Or something more substantial,' she added. 'How long have you got?'

Taken by surprise, he said, 'I need to be back by five o'clock.'

She thrust the treats back into his hand, and he jumped when her fingers brushed his palm, the unexpected contact unnerving him.

He said, 'It's okay, I'll grab something on the way—'

'Will avocado on toast with a poached egg be okay?'

'Um...' He'd never eaten avocado, although Clare used to like them.

'Get Bertie in the crate, and I'll make you a snack. Deal?'

Jakob continued to hesitate.

'I was going to make myself something anyway. I'll just make a bit extra. It's no biggie, honestly.'

'Um, okay. Thanks.' He wished he could stop saying *um*. 'I do feel peckish. Forgot to eat lunch.'

She smiled ruefully. 'I do that sometimes.' Then she was gone again, into the kitchen, leaving him to tempt Bertie into the crate.

Bertie knew something was up, and although Jakob could tell that the dog desperately wanted the treat, he was reluctant to venture inside. Yep, it was going to take a while to convince Bertie not to be such a Velcro dog. He seemed to have become quite attached to Gretta in just a few days, but it was understandable since his entire world had been turned upside down and she was the only constant. No wonder the little guy was so anxious.

Just before Gretta called him to come eat, her cat crept warily into the sitting room, and Jakob sat back on his haunches, waiting for Zaza to approach. Bertie, he noticed, was careful to keep a respectful distance. The dog wasn't scared, but he was cautious, and Jakob was gratified to see that they were cohabiting without any aggro. He had no doubt that the cat had the upper hand, though.

Zaza studied him before deciding he was no threat, and that the treats Jakob held in his hand needed investigating. Jakob gave her one; then, in the interest of fairness, he gave one to Bertie.

'It's ready, if you want to go wash your hands,' Gretta called, and when he sat at the table, his hands damp and smelling of the nice soap she used, she placed a plate in front of him.

'Did he get in it?' she asked.

'Not a chance.' Bertie, Jakob noticed, was sitting on her foot in the hope that something tasty would come his way. Zaza, though, seemed less interested in food, and more interested in rubbing her face against his leg.

'It's like he knows what's going on,' Gretta grumbled.

'He's a bright boy, so he probably does.' Jakob popped a forkful of food into his mouth. 'Mmm, this is good,' then he added, 'I feel a fraud, since the deal was that you feed me if I get him to go into the crate.'

'You warned me it would take a while,' she reminded him.

Silence followed as they ate, and Jakob wondered whether he should try to fill it. But the problem was, he wasn't sure what to say. He didn't do small talk. He never had. Talking about dogs, the other animals in the rescue centre, or the various aspects of his job was easy. Anything else he struggled with.

Gretta didn't seem keen on idle chat either, and it occurred to him that she might feel just as self-conscious. He wasn't entirely sure what her job entailed, but if she worked from home maybe she was out of practice when it came to general chit-chat.

'Do you get lonely?' he blurted, without thinking.

'Excuse me?' She looked affronted, and he hoped he hadn't upset her.

'Working from home. I've read that it can be lonely.'

'I've got Zaza.'

He nodded vigorously, to show that he knew what she meant. His dogs were brilliant company, although he did sometimes miss—

Bugger! He was thinking about Clare again. He really wished he would stop doing that, especially since he didn't miss *her* as such. He missed what they'd had. What he'd *thought* they'd had. Although, they clearly *hadn't* had it, because if they'd had, she wouldn't have had an affair. *Affairs*. Plural.

'It's been five days,' Gretta said. 'Only two more, then if no one comes forward, will you put him up for adoption?'

Jakob was surprised how disappointed he felt. He was right: she couldn't wait to be rid of the dog.

'It's just...' She hesitated. 'What if it takes longer than a week to find Mr Butler's relatives? I mean, they could be on holiday, or living abroad...?'

'Are you suggesting we should wait a while?'

'Is that possible?'

Jakob studied her face, trying to decipher her expression. Was it hope he saw? 'We could, if it's in his best interests.' He finished the last mouthful of food.

'Would it be?'

'It depends.'

'On what?'

'On how attached he becomes. He's started to bond with you.'

'That's a good thing, right?'

'Not if he's decided that you're his human. He'll be devastated all over again when it's time for him to leave. The sooner we find him his forever home, the better it'll be for him.'

And with that, Jakob took his leave. He had to go to work because there were other dogs who needed his love and attention.

But all the time he was there, and long into the night, he had Gretta and Bertie on his mind.

CHAPTER NINE

THERE'S SOMETHING *very wrong with this scenario*, Gretta mused from inside the dog crate, as she gazed out at Bertie. He was panting. Or grinning. She wasn't sure which. Grinning, probably.

No wonder. He must think her a right wally, especially since she'd given him the treat anyway without him having to climb inside. She'd wriggled into it, to show him there was nothing to fear.

Zaza had stalked off in disgust, and frankly Gretta didn't blame her. Bertie was making a total fool of her.

Oh, well, she sighed, as she clambered out of it with difficulty, groaning as she straightened up, her back aching and her limbs cramping. She wasn't surprised he didn't like the crate: she didn't, either.

'We'll try again later,' she promised. 'This isn't going to go away. You'll have to get used to it. Now, if you were a good boy,' she continued in a conversational tone, 'and didn't make so much of a fuss when you're left on your own, you wouldn't need to be crated in the first place. It's ridiculous, Bertie; I can't even have a wee without you following me to the loo. You don't see Zaza being such a baby. And what am I doing, talking to you like you can understand me?'

Bertie was sitting at her feet, staring up at her, his head tilted to one side, his ears pricked. He really did look as though he understood every word. His eyes gazed deeply into hers, and she wondered what was going on in his furry little head. What was he thinking? How was he feeling?

Gretta was surprised how much she cared. He was rather cute and extremely loving, and when she recalled the exuberant welcome he'd given her when she'd fetched him from Mr Butler's house after she'd been shopping earlier, her heart melted.

Gretta was just debating whether to do some work for an hour or two before she called it a night, when her phone rang.

It was her older sister.

Gretta hesitated before answering, wondering what Taylor wanted, and it briefly occurred to her to let it go to voicemail, but decided against it. 'Hi.'

'What's going on, Gretta? Why are you avoiding everyone?' Her sister's tone was abrupt.

'I'm not.' Her reply was defensive. And untruthful.

'You most definitely are. And don't say you're too busy, because I don't believe you.'

'I *am* busy.' Gretta bit her lip.

'Doing what?'

'Working.' It sounded the weak excuse that it was. She was busy because she *wanted* to be; because it filled the empty spaces in her life. She could easily make time for her family. But they'd made their indifference towards her clear.

Taylor was only phoning out of a sense of duty. Gretta as the middle child, had always been invisible, unnoticed for the most part, sandwiched as she was between strong, forthright, opinionated Taylor and flighty, oddball, exuberant Sienna.

Looking back, she realised that Landon had taken advantage of that, and it had been all too easy to segregate her from them. It had been gradual and insidious, of course, because that's the way people like Landon operated.

She'd slowly but surely disappeared from her family's lives, and they hadn't noticed. And what was really sad was that Gretta would be happy not to be noticed by anyone ever again. Being noticed led to heartbreak.

A bark made her jump, and she realised Bertie was trying to get her attention.

'What was that?' Taylor demanded. 'Have you got *a dog?*'

Bertie barked again. He was in the hall, and Gretta followed him out to see what all the fuss was about.

'Sort of. Not really. The old guy next door died, and I'm taking care of it for a few days.'

As she was talking, Gretta put her eye to the peephole, but there was no one at the door. With a sigh, she went upstairs. After this phone call, losing herself in work for the rest of the evening would be a good idea.

'I didn't think you liked dogs,' her sister said.

Neither did Gretta – until she'd been landed with Bertie. 'I've got a cat, too.'

'Wow! I thought you hated cats.'

'*Landon* hated cats,' she replied shortly. She'd always wanted a cat.

Bertie let out a volley of barks, and she realised he hadn't come upstairs with her. Then she heard a door slam and abruptly she knew what had set him off. *Someone was next door!*

'I've got to go,' she said, vaguely hearing Taylor's cry of, 'Wait, can you—' before cutting her off.

However, by the time she made it outside, whoever had been in Mr Butler's house had gone.

And so had the note.

'FLIPPIN' HECK, THIS dog is seriously trying my patience,' Gretta grumbled as she scoured the garden. She'd only taken her eyes off Bertie for a minute and he'd disappeared.

Ah, there he was, peeping out from around a bush. He slunk towards her, looking dejected.

Hearing someone next door and then having Gretta leave him on his own while she went to investigate (he hadn't strictly been alone because Zaza had still been in the house, and it had only been for a few minutes), had unsettled him all over again, just when Gretta had got him onto an even keel of sorts.

When she'd returned, he'd paced around the house whining, and every so often he'd go to the door and give it a desultory scratch. So when he'd asked to go out for a wee, she'd let him into the garden, grateful for a brief respite from the dog's restlessness.

At first, she'd kept a beady eye on him, but she'd began to fume as her thoughts turned to the person who had entered Mr Butler's house, read her note, and ignored the dog's plight. And *hers*, for that matter. Whoever it was had taken it for granted that she'd continue to look after the dog. Or worse – they hadn't given her a second thought.

Gretta snorted angrily. She should be used to that by now. Her family had been guilty of not giving her a second thought for years. If ever. No wonder she'd—

Gretta shook her head to clear it. Trying to be charitable, she put herself in this unknown relative's shoes. Maybe they weren't in a position to relieve her of Bertie. But if that was the case, they should at least have let her know. And now she was back to being cross again.

She wondered what Jakob would say when she told him, and she guessed he would be just as annoyed. Admittedly, it would be more on Bertie's behalf than hers. For Jakob, animals came first, humans a very poor second.

She got the feeling he didn't mind her though, and maybe even liked her, despite them getting off on the wrong foot when they'd first met. She'd thought him grumpy, brusque and rather rude. And she guessed he must have thought her clueless or negligent. Both, perhaps.

Even if she said so herself, her dog knowledge had come a long way in a week. And most of that was due to Jakob and his patience with her. He was a fount of knowledge, and incredibly patient when it came to canine welfare. At first glance he appeared to be a big rough bear of a man, but she'd seen firsthand how gentle and kind he could be.

Surprised, Gretta realised that she genuinely liked him. He was the only man she'd allowed into her life since Landon, and she was beginning to regard him as a friend. An *attractive* friend.

Disconcerted, she gave herself a mental shake. It didn't matter how attractive she found him, or how nice he was, she wasn't going there. Never again would she allow a man to get close enough to hurt her. Never again would she trust anyone the way she'd trusted Landon. At least, in *the beginning* she had trusted him. Later, the only thing she trusted him to do was hurt her. And he'd done a pretty good job of that.

When she'd finally gathered what was left of herself and walked out, she'd vowed she'd never be in that position again. She'd hated being so vulnerable. Anyone would. Which was probably why she'd felt so much sympathy for little Bertie.

Actually...where *was* Bertie? She couldn't see him anywhere.

'Bertie? Bertie? Come here, there's a good boy. Bertie!'

The dog remained conspicuously absent.

'*Bertie!*' she shouted louder; not a cajoling call, but a command.

No response.

He must be hiding. He couldn't have got out because she'd blocked the hole up, and she began to search the garden, pushing shrubs aside and probing under bushes. Then she saw it. The little sod had dug another hole. He'd got under the fence and was undoubtedly in Mr Butler's garden.

With a resigned sigh, she went to retrieve him. *Again.*

Then she phoned Jakob to let him know about the visitor next door.

'Someone was in Mr Butler's house earlier,' she said. 'I don't know who, I didn't see. I was on the phone with my sister and didn't realise until too late. The note's gone though, so they might contact the kennels. I thought I'd give you the heads up.'

'Thanks. I'll keep an eye out, and I'll tell Maisie and the others.'

'It was Bertie who alerted me. He must have thought Mr Butler had come back.' There was a hitch in her voice as she said it. 'After I'd gone round to check, I realised he'd escaped again. He'd dug another hole under the fence, and I found him in Mr Butler's garden sitting on the step. It was so sad. What if they don't bother collecting him? What if they're happy for him to be re-homed?'

The answer was obvious, and she wasn't sure she could handle that.

Gretta had a decision to make.

TAKING BERTIE OUT for a walk had become something Gretta quite looked forward to and rather enjoyed. Mind you, the weather recently had been pretty good, so she hadn't yet been forced to take him out in the rain.

She'd been on pins the following morning, fully expecting a phone call from Jakob to tell her that someone had been in touch with him about Bertie. However, her phone had remained silent, and she'd managed to get some work done.

It was time for a break, though. Bertie had been very good, snoozing by her feet, but he'd become restless in the last ten minutes and she guessed he wanted a change of scenery. A good walk now would earn her a few hours' peace this afternoon, so she decided to take him on a similar walk to the one she'd taken him with Jakob and his dogs the other day, but maybe not quite as far.

Bertie danced around her legs as she got ready, putting her shoes on and grabbing a lightweight jacket. And he practically bounced with excitement when she put his harness on him and attached the lead. Making sure she had her phone, she set off, striding along the pavement, the dog trotting at her side.

She'd only just made it to the high street when an elderly woman stopped her.

'Excuse me, but aren't you the young lady who lives next door to Mr Butler?'

Gretta blinked, wondering what she wanted. 'Yes...?' she replied cautiously.

'I recognised Bertie,' the woman said, 'and I heard his neighbour was looking after him. How has he been? Missing him, I bet.'

Bertie wagged his bottom at the lady, his tongue lolling out of the side of his mouth.

'You know me, don't you, Bertie? I give you bits of biscuit.' She turned back to Gretta. 'Mr Butler used to pop into the cafe twice a week for a cuppa, and Bertie was always with him. He never went anywhere without his dog.' She pinned Gretta with a beady eye. 'Have you heard when the funeral is?'

'No, have you?'

The woman shook her head. 'I was hoping you might, since you're looking after his dog. I'd like to pay my respects. I've been keeping an eye on the newsagent's window. They sometimes post funeral notices in there. Anyway, I'd better get on. I've got an appointment about my bunions. Bye, Bertie, be good for...what's your name? Gretta, isn't it?'

'That's right.'

'I'm Ada Manning. Nice to meet you, Gretta.'

'You too, Mrs Manning.'

'It's Miss. Never could be doing with having a bloke around. Too much trouble, if you ask me.' And with that, she was off, leaving Gretta gazing at her retreating back in amusement.

But Miss Manning had the right idea – men *were* too much trouble. Most of them. Jakob appeared to be the exception to the rule.

She wondered whether she'd bump into him on the walk. Then a thought gave her pause: was *that* why she was going in this direction? Previous walks had been around the field behind her house. Short walks, where she'd hardly seen anyone, not even another dog walker.

Another thought occurred to her: did Bertie miss other dogs? Should she walk him in places where he was more likely to meet a doggy friend or two? She recalled how well he'd got on with Jakob's dogs and the little foster dog, Trixie. Was a lack of canine interaction harming him? He seemed to be quite a sociable little chap, happy to greet everyone.

Whereas she was not. Aside from the occasional online call with clients, and the necessary interaction with staff when she went shopping, Gretta sometimes didn't speak to anyone for days. Yet, since she'd acquired Bertie, she'd spoken to more people in a week than she'd done in a month. Take yesterday, for instance: she'd had a visit from Jakob, then she'd spoken to him again on the phone after she'd had a call from her sister...

Gretta didn't want to think about her sister or the rest of her family, but she found she couldn't banish the intrusive thoughts. They kept slipping into her mind whenever it wasn't occupied. Like now, for instance. She should try to think about something else.

Jakob: she'd think about *Jakob*. Or rather, she'd think about the next step he might suggest in trying to crate-train the little menace. Aside from shoving Bertie inside and shutting the door on him, she didn't know what else to try, and she was damn sure she wasn't going to risk leaving him alone in the kitchen. He'd wreaked enough havoc the last time, and she'd only been upstairs. Imagine the damage he could cause if she was out of the house?

At least he and Zaza were getting on, she said to herself, as she left the village behind and slipped through the kissing gate at the start of the path leading to the stables and the farm beyond. She'd heard the farm had a shop selling all kinds of fresh produce, so that was her destination. She'd check it out, maybe make a purchase or two, then spend the rest of the day creating a series of promotional social media posts for an author whose book was due to be published in a couple of months. Hopefully, Bertie would be worn out and would sleep until supper time.

The trudge up the hill was steeper than she remembered, and she was puffing and panting by the time she turned into the farmyard. Thinking back to her walk with Jakob the other day, she realised he'd hardly been out of breath at all. It must be all that dog walking he did, keeping him fit. If Gretta got nothing else out of looking after Bertie, at least she'd be a little fitter. The problem with having a sedentary job was that she had to make an effort to exercise, and she'd always had a tendency to take the path of least resistance. But the 'anything for an easy life' mentality was what had got her into a mess, because Landon had shamelessly and systematically exploited that. *And she'd let him.*

'Hi, can I help you?' a woman asked, and Gretta realised she'd come to a breathless halt in the middle of the farmyard.

'I was looking for the farm shop,' she said, her chest heaving.

'It's over there.' The woman pointed to a doorway with a sign saying 'Farm Shop' above it. 'Have you walked up the lane?'

Gretta nodded, feeling foolish.

'It's a bit of a trek, isn't it?' The woman gazed at Bertie. 'There's a bowl of water by the door if he fancies a drink.'

'Okay, thanks.'

'Do you live in the village?'

'Foxglove Street.'

'My sister lives there! Nicki Warring. She's got a little boy, Sammy. Her partner is Gio; he's a police officer.'

'You're not Maisie Fairfax?' Gretta was confused.

'That's my other sister. She owns The Forever Home Boarding Kennels. I'm Dulcie.'

Dulcie looked at her expectantly, so Gretta said, 'I'm Gretta, and this is Bertie.' After she'd said it, she felt daft introducing the dog.

Dulcie said, 'That wouldn't be Bertie Butler, would it?'

Gretta blinked. 'It would.'

'Maisie told me all about him. The poor little soul. Good on you for taking him in.'

Gretta didn't know what to say to that, so she simply smiled and didn't say anything.

As though sensing her discomfort, Dulcie said, 'Sorry, I'm keeping you talking. Just go on in; Bea will help if you've got any questions. By the way, this week's ice cream flavour is dandelion. It's surprisingly good.' She laughed, and Gretta guessed that her incredulity must be reflected on her face. Whoever heard of dandelion ice cream!

'It's got a honey-like flavour,' Dulcie was saying. 'Ask Bea for a taste and see for yourself. Nice to meet you, Gretta. You too, Bertie.'

That was the second random person she'd spoken to today because of Bertie, Gretta mused as she went into the shop.

If this carried on, in a few more weeks she'd have made the acquaintance of everyone in Picklewick.

The thought didn't fill her with the alarm she assumed it would. Bertie, it seemed, was bringing her out of her shell.

Maybe she was *finally* beginning to heal.

CHAPTER TEN

'CAN YOU HEAR THAT?' Gretta demanded, holding her phone up.

*Aaawooohooo...*Bertie yodelled.

Jakob was laughing.

'It's not funny,' she told him crossly. If she was going to keep Bertie, she needed to get this sorted. And she definitely *was* going to keep him. Whoever had been in Mr Butler's house the other day hadn't stepped forward to claim him, so...

'He's got a good set of lungs on him,' Jakob said.

'I'm only in the hall,' she protested. 'I haven't even left the house yet.'

'How long has he been in his crate?'

Gretta did a quick calculation. 'One minute and six seconds.'

'It's a start.'

'Not a very good one.'

'You might want to go back to the kitchen and let him know you haven't left the country,' he suggested.

As soon as she opened the kitchen door, the noise abruptly ceased and Bertie glared at her accusingly.

'He's giving me a look,' she told Jakob. 'I feel dreadful.'

'Let him out and I guarantee he'll be all over you.'

Gretta unlatched the crate and Bertie bounded out, leaping up at her and almost sending her flying. He was uttering little whimpers of relief.

'How long did you say this would take?' she asked.

'How long is a piece of string?'

'Great. I'll never be able to leave the house without him.'

Jakob was laughing again. 'You're being rather dramatic.'

'You heard him,' she argued.

'How did you get him in there?'

'I didn't. He went in by himself when I wasn't looking.' She was quite aggrieved by that. All her tempting and cajoling had been in vain. He'd entered the crate in his own sweet time, and not before.

'And then what did you do?' Jakob asked.

'I shut him in and went outside. Except, I didn't get as far as *outside*. I only got to the hall before he started howling.'

'You've missed a couple of steps and gone too fast,' Jakob said.

'What should I have done?'

'Let him get used to going in and out of the crate freely for a day or so.'

'Oh, heck. He's going to think it's a prison, isn't he? He's not going to go anywhere near it again.'

'Shall I bring Trixie over? She's happy in a crate. It's her safe place. If he sees another dog using it, he mightn't be so worried.'

'I don't want to be a nuisance.' Gretta realised that once again she was calling on Jakob for help and he probably had better things to do than come running whenever she was in a pickle.

'You're not being a nuisance. I'll be with you in half an hour.'

When he arrived, Bertie was delighted to see that he had Trixie with him, and he bounced around her, wagging his backside, but not before he'd given Jakob an equally enthusiastic welcome.

Gretta said, 'Thanks, I really appreciate this. It's getting to be a habit, you popping in on your way to or from work.'

'It's my day off today. I was at home.'

Ah, that explains why he had Trixie with him. Gretta felt even worse now. 'I wish you'd told me. It could have waited until tomorrow, or the next day.'

'I wanted to come,' he replied, and an unexpectedly warm glow suffused her cheeks – until he added, 'Trixie could use some more socialising. She needs more exposure to new people and different situations.'

Gretta might have known...

'Do all dogs like you?' she asked as Bertie continued to make a fuss of him.

'Not all, no. Most, though.'

His attention was on the dogs. Gretta's was on *him*.

He filled her sitting room with his calm presence. Despite his size (or maybe because of it) she felt safe with him around. Which was an odd way to feel after what she'd been through with a man of far less impressive stature than Jakob; she would have expected to be wary of him. But she wasn't.

Was that because Bertie and the distressingly timid Trixie both adored him? Animals had sharper instincts than humans, didn't they? Or was that an old wives' tale?

Trixie kept close to Jakob, Gretta noticed, after the dog had given her a cautious sniff, but she didn't push it. According to Jakob, she'd probably been abused or neglected, or both, and was distrustful of people.

'It might be an idea to move the crate into the sitting room,' Jakob suggested.

Gretta had transferred it to the kitchen, because that's where she assumed dogs should be kept when their owners weren't around. She also thought that's where they should sleep at night. But Bertie had had other ideas, and although she'd managed to persuade him not to jump up on her bed and sleep with his head on her pillow, he'd still insisted on sleeping in her bedroom. So she'd made a kind of cosy nest for him by the side of her dressing table, which Zaza was far happier about. Her cat hadn't been too keen on sharing Gretta's bed with the dog, either.

'Why the sitting room?' Gretta wanted to know.

'Because it's a place for chilling out and relaxing, and that's what you want him to do in his crate.'

It made sense, so she found a space for it where it wasn't in the way.

'Do you have an old throw or a blanket to drape over it?' he asked, explaining that covering it over would give it a more den-like vibe. 'He needs to know that this is his safe place, that he won't be disturbed.' He put a few of Bertie's toys in it while she dug out a throw. 'There, that should do it.'

'Now what?'

'I'm going to persuade Trixie to get in it and hopefully Bertie will follow.' Jakob produced a plastic tub from his pocket. 'Chicken,' he announced.

Trixie's ears pricked up and Bertie's nose twitched. Even Zaza, who'd been keeping a reserved distance on the back of the sofa, seemed to sense there were goodies on offer.

Jakob opened it with a flourish, took out a piece and pretended to eat, murmuring 'Yum, yum,' as he did so.

Gretta pressed her lips together, trying not to smile.

'If they think it's yours, they'll want it even more,' he explained, giving a bit to Trixie.

Bertie was crestfallen but perked up when Jakob gave him a piece, too.

'Can you hold him for a minute?' he asked.

Gretta sat on the floor and wrapped her arms around Bertie's chunky little body, and he licked her cheek, his breath chickeny. 'Ew, stop that!' she cried, rubbing her face against her arm.

'He loves you,' Jakob chuckled. 'Doggy kisses are the best.'

Gretta had no idea why, but her eyes immediately strayed to Jakob's mouth and she wondered what it would be like to be kissed by *him*. Shocked, she hastily dropped her gaze. It landed on his large hands, and an image of them on her body made her gasp.

Nuh-uh, she wasn't going to go there. She didn't need another man in her life. *Ever.*

Thankfully Jakob's attention was on Trixie and not her, so he hadn't noticed her sudden discomfort.

Gretta tried to concentrate on holding Bertie still, as Jakob threw a morsel of chicken into the back of the crate. Trixie looked from Jakob to the crate, then back again.

'It's okay,' he assured her. 'You can go in.' To Gretta, he said, 'She's been in this crate before, so it should still have her scent.'

Nervously, and with a false start or two, Trixie crept inside.

Bertie wriggled furiously, indignant that she was getting another piece of chicken and he wasn't. Trixie emerged, licking her lips.

'You can let him go,' Jakob instructed, and when Gretta released him Bertie darted up to Trixie and sniffed. Then he gave Jakob a reproachful look.

'Do you want some? Is Trixie getting all the treats? If you want more chicken you're going to have to go get it,' Jakob told him, tossing a piece into the back of the crate.

Bertie didn't hesitate; he shot inside and gobbled it down. He was soon back out again though, obviously not keen to linger.

Gretta leant back against the sofa watching Jakob. Her eyes lingered on his face, his kind eyes, the curve of his nose, while he repeated the process a few more times until he eventually called time.

'The crate may stop him from tearing my door to shreds,' Gretta said, 'but how will it stop him howling?'

'It won't. That's a separate issue. I'll show you now, if you like?'

She nodded, eager to do anything to curb Bertie's wailing, and with a bit of encouragement, Jakob persuaded both dogs to enter the crate, then closed the door. Bertie immediately started to whine and scrabble.

Gretta shot Jakob an anxious look, then told herself that she had to trust him to know what he was doing.

*Trust...*It was a concept she hadn't been familiar with for a long time.

'What now?' she asked.

'Put the kettle on and we'll have a cup of tea.'

Frowning, she went into the kitchen and made the drinks. When she returned, Jakob was sitting on the sofa and the dogs were curled up together in the crate.

Taking a mug from her with a smile, he said, 'They seem nice and settled, so we'll drink this then we'll go outside for a minute.'

As she sat down to drink hers, it struck Gretta how normal this was. There was no hidden agenda (well, there *was*, but it was aimed at Bertie, not her). There was no side to Jakob. He didn't play mind games or try to manipulate and control. She realised she was beginning to think of him as a friend, and she hadn't had one of those in a long time. But was this friendship based solely on dogs?

Of course it was, she told herself. The only thing they had in common was concern for Bertie.

To make conversation and avoid an awkward silence (awkward for her, that is, because Jakob seemed perfectly happy with not talking), she said, 'I took Bertie for a walk to the farm earlier. Met Dulcie, Maisie's sister. Just how many of them are there?'

'Four, I believe; five if you count their mother. She lives in the cottage halfway up Muddypuddle Lane. The three sisters live in Picklewick and there's a brother who lives in New Zealand.'

As they chatted for a white about The Forever Home and the farm, Zaza climbed onto Jakob's lap and lay there purring. With the two dogs asleep, it was quite a peaceful domestic scene, and Gretta found herself relaxing more than she thought possible. Jakob was an easy man to have around.

She would have been happy to sit for a while longer, but he gently placed the cat on a cushion and got up. Gretta stared up at him.

'Let's go into the hall for a minute,' he said. 'No fuss, just stand up and walk quietly out of the room.'

Rising, Gretta shot Bertie a quick look. His ears were pricked and he was watching her, but Trixie hadn't reacted, so he didn't either. It was a start.

It was also a false sense of security, because the second Gretta stepped out of the room, he whined. Jakob suggested she went back in and comforted him, which she did with alacrity, hating to hear Bertie upset. Trixie was also looking worried, so Jakob scooped her into his arms and cuddled her.

'Okay,' Jakob said, putting the terrier down. 'He's going to need more desensitisation. What I suggest is that you wait until he's settled and preferably tired, then you keep getting up and walking about. Get him used to you moving around, and he'll gradually understand that it's not necessary for him to follow you every time. Go to the door, but don't leave the room, then go back to your chair, and once he's happy with that and doesn't react—' Jakob stopped.

'What?'

'That's enough to be going on with. You've both made loads of progress today. I'll pop by again in a day or so. Bye, Bertie.' He strode into the hall, Trixie at his heels, and opened the front door.

Gretta and Bertie followed. 'Thanks. You don't know how much I appreciate this. I'm sure Bertie does too...'

She stopped talking as movement on the other side of the street caught her attention.

Her eyes widened and her heart sank like a stone in a pond. It was someone she knew only too well.

Landon!

She inhaled sharply, and might have made some kind of noise, because Jakob turned to follow her gaze.

Gretta froze. She couldn't move. Her eyes were glued to the man walking along the opposite side of the street. How had he—? Why was he—?

Oh, God, *it wasn't him,* she realised suddenly, sagging against the door frame. She'd been so convinced, and shock had rendered her immobile.

Then relief made her burst into tears.

JAKOB GLARED AT THE MAN, wondering what he'd done to Gretta to cause such a reaction. But despite his urge to go rushing after the bloke and confront him, it was more important he took care of Gretta.

As he ushered her back inside, Jakob made sure the guy was walking away, then he closed the door firmly and accompanied her into the sitting room. Even as he wondered whether he was doing the right thing, he knew he couldn't leave her like this.

He could see her shoulders shaking and he stepped forward, his hand outstretched, before he dropped it to his side; he wasn't a touchy-feely person, unless it was an animal. 'Gretta? Are you okay?'

She had her back to him, and he wished he could see her face as she said, 'I'm fine.'

'Who was he?'

'No one.' Bertie was sitting at Gretta's feet, his little face worried. He kept tapping her leg with his nose, but she ignored him.

'If he's no one, why are you crying?'

She took a deep breath and sniffed before she turned to face him, dabbing at the skin under her eyes with the pads of her fingers. 'I thought he was someone else,' she said shakily, 'but I was wrong.'

'Are you in trouble?'

'No.'

'Danger?'

'No.' She blinked furiously. 'I need a drink.'

'Would you like me to make some tea?'

'An *alcoholic* drink. I've got a bottle of wine around here somewhere.' She went into the kitchen and Bertie trotted after her, then stopped, looked back at Jakob and whined again.

Jakob took the hint. 'I'm not leaving until I know you're alright,' he called.

She reappeared with two glasses and a bottle of red. 'In that case, you can help me drink this.'

'I'm driving.'

Gretta seemed to fold in on herself. 'Oh, yes, of course.'

He relented. 'I'll just have the one, if that's okay?'

'Thanks. I'm not usually this pathetic. It was just my...family...they don't know. I didn't tell them.' She unscrewed the top and poured the wine.

Jakob winced as it glugged into the glasses; Gretta wasn't stingy with her measures. He'd better take care to drink only half of that.

'I'm not making sense, am I?' she said.

'Not much.'

After taking a gulp of the ruby liquid, she scooped Bertie up and gave him a cuddle. The dog looked relieved, and when she put him down again, he trotted off in search of Trixie, who had retreated to the crate, the upset making her anxious.

Gretta sat down and Jakob took the armchair next to her. 'I thought the man outside was my ex,' she said.

'Husband?'

She shook her head. 'We weren't married, thank goodness.'

Jakob could guess what was coming, and his blood began to boil. The little things he'd noticed, such as her careful looks up and down the street, and the way she made sure to lock her front door...She was *scared.*

But what she told him next wasn't what he'd expected.

'Landon wasn't violent, if that's what you're thinking. He never laid a finger on me. But he hurt me, all the same. He was incredibly controlling, but before you say anything, he wasn't like that when we first met. It was gradual, insidious, and by the time alarm bells were ringing, he'd isolated me from my family and my friends. I didn't even go out to work because he didn't like it. I worked from home.'

'Your family...?' His question was hesitant. He didn't want to pry.

'I've got two sisters. I'm the middle one. Do you have any brothers or sisters?'

'A brother. He's five years older than me.'

'Then you probably won't understand.'

'Try me.'

'There's something called middle child syndrome, characterised by the child feeling ignored, overlooked, not as important as the first-born or the baby of the family. They tend to have a sense of not belonging, yet they have a drive to prove themselves. In other words, they're screwed up. That's me, in a nutshell.' She swirled the wine around in her glass, but didn't drink any. 'Which is why I haven't told my parents or my sisters what Landon did, how he treated me.'

'Wouldn't they want to know?'

'I'm not sure they'd be all that interested, if I'm honest.'

Jakob wasn't into uttering platitudes such as 'I'm sure they would be' and as a result he didn't know how best to comfort her, or even whether she'd want him to. If a dog was in distress, he knew what to do: but with a human, not so much.

'I'm sorry,' she said. 'You didn't need to hear all that.' She stared at her drink. 'I don't know why I told you.'

Neither did Jakob, but he was glad she had. 'Don't be sorry. I'd hate to think of you upset and on your own.'

A small smile spread across Gretta's face and she pointed to Bertie, who was watching her with loving eyes.

She said, 'I've just come to realise that I'm not on my own, not when I have Bertie. Bless him, he was so concerned.'

'Dogs can be very sensitive to their owner's feelings.'

The smile grew. She opened her mouth, closed it again, then said, 'I want to keep him.'

Jakob was overjoyed. 'I was hoping you might. He clearly adores you. Now *that's* a cause for celebration.' He raised his glass and took a teeny mouthful.

He noticed that she only sipped at hers, and didn't gulp it as he feared. She seemed calmer, as though the act of telling him, of sharing what had happened to her, had released some of the tension.

Would it be okay to leave her now? He really did have to get back.

'Are you going to be alright if I go?' he asked, although he was beginning to realise that he'd be quite happy to stay for as long as she would allow him to. If it wasn't for Stan and Ripley...

'I'm fine. It was the shock.'

'Are you scared of him?'

She shook her head firmly. 'No. As I said, he was never violent. I moved to Picklewick so I wouldn't risk bumping into him. The memories are bad enough, without having to see him in the flesh.'

She got to her feet, and he took it as his cue to leave, placing his barely touched glass of wine on the side table.

'You've got my number if you need me,' he said, 'and I don't mean just for problems with Bertie. You can ring me anytime, okay?'

'Okay.' She gave him a watery smile. 'Thanks for everything.'

'You're welcome.' Strolling ahead of her to the door, he stopped suddenly and turned around, remembering Trixie, and as he did so Gretta walked straight into him.

Reflexively his arms went around her to steady her, and he wasn't sure how it happened or who made the first move, but suddenly his lips met hers and they were kissing.

Jakob closed his eyes as he explored her mouth. Her arms wound around his neck and a rush of desire caught him unawares, jabbing him in the stomach, making him groan.

The noise brought him to his senses.

What was he doing?

His eyes snapped open and he pulled away at the same time as she did, and he stared at her in dismay.

Gretta's expression was one of horror. She was equally aghast.

And Bertie's worried whimper said it all.

CHAPTER ELEVEN

THE DOG WAS A BOUNCY, friendly German Shepherd cross, who was desperate to run after his ball – although he wasn't as keen on bringing it back. He was currently standing in the middle of the enclosed field at The Forever Home, his tail waving from side to side, his eyes bright and hopeful, and a neon pink ball wedged in his mouth.

'You've got to let me have it, if you want me to throw it again,' Jakob told him.

Another wag of the tail, but no movement on the ball-dropping front, and Jakob shook his head, amused.

Determined not to let go of his prize, the dog trotted off for a sniff, leaving Jakob alone with his thoughts, which was something he'd tried desperately to avoid doing since he'd left Gretta's house yesterday.

Unfortunately, he hadn't been successful. Even after mulling it over and over for most of the night, he wasn't sure how Gretta had come to be in his arms.

His lips still tingled. To be honest, *all* of him still tingled. For a few wonderful, magical moments he'd lost himself to the sensations flooding through him: the taste of her lips, her light flowery scent, the feel of her body against his.

And then he'd come to his senses and jerked away, mortified.

Fancying her was one thing, acting on it was another, and all because he'd been thrilled that she'd fallen in love with Bertie and wanted to give him a forever home. That was no reason to kiss her, especially since he'd vowed never to let anyone get under his skin again. Once bitten...

Maybe one day he'd be able to face risking his heart again, but not yet. Clare's betrayal was still too raw, too recent.

Some people might say that three years was long enough to get over the way she'd treated him, but he'd loved her. And love didn't have a switch to be turned on and off. It wasn't something to be controlled. He might hate what she'd done and the way she'd behaved, but he hadn't been able to hate *her*.

Jakob wished he hadn't kissed Gretta, but there was no putting the genie back in the bottle, and now he couldn't stop thinking about her.

Should he phone and apologise, or would it make things worse?

If he'd intended to apologise, he should have done so straight away, but he'd called Trixie to him and had left with a muttered goodbye, a body that was on fire, and a mind in turmoil.

How did Gretta feel about it? Had she forgiven him? Her expression had been one of dismay, but for a few delicious moments she'd thrown herself into the kiss, and he was sure she'd been swept away by its intensity, just as he had.

Could he pretend it had never happened?

Possibly, if he kept his distance.

He should ask Dawn to handle the adoption paperwork. He needn't get involved.

Gretta might appreciate that, because she had her own emotional baggage to contend with, and he doubted she needed any more.

The dog, bored with sniffing, sidled up to him and dropped the ball at his feet. Jakob threw it, and as the animal bounded joyfully after it, Jakob kept coming back to how good the kiss had felt. How right. And how much he liked Gretta as a person. As a *woman*.

And how much Clare had hurt him.

He hadn't got over how she'd treated him, and he wasn't sure he ever would. And now she was back in town, dredging up memories he'd worked hard to bury.

The dog was panting hard after finally getting the idea that dropping the ball so it could be thrown again meant more fun, and Jakob deemed him tired enough to return him to his pen for a nap.

He was giving his ears a final ruffle and telling him what a good boy he was, when Jakob heard his name being called.

Slipping out of the kennel, he secured the door, then looked at Maisie. She had a woman with her.

'Jakob, this is Erica Hilliard. She's here about the French bulldog, Bertie, the one whose owner died and—'

'I know the one,' he broke in, making her blink in surprise at his rudeness.

The woman also appeared uncertain, glancing from him to Maisie and back again. She said, 'He was my uncle. I'm sorry, but I didn't know he had a dog until a few days ago. I would have come sooner, but there's so much to do when someone dies.' She put a hand to her cheek. 'At least the funeral is sorted now. It's a week Thursday in Thornbury Church.' She glanced up and down the row of kennels. 'Can I take the dog now?'

'He's not here,' Jakob told her gruffly, a barrage of emotions sweeping over him, the most prominent being dismay for Gretta. She was going to be so upset.

'Please don't tell me he's been re-homed already,' Erica said. 'I don't think my uncle would have wanted it to go to strangers.'

Jakob bit back a retort. How could she know what Mr Butler wanted, if she hadn't even known he'd had a dog? They couldn't have been close.

'He's being fostered,' Jakob said, trying to keep his voice neutral. Mr Butler's relationship with his family wasn't his concern; Bertie's welfare and the law, *was.*

What about Gretta? a little voice in his head asked. *Aren't you concerned about her?*

He was actually. *Very* concerned. This would devastate her.

'What does that mean?' Erica asked.

'He didn't settle in kennels, so someone is looking after him in their home.'

'Oh, I see. Can I go fetch him?'

Jakob sighed. He had little choice. She was entitled to take the dog. 'Let me give Gretta a call, make sure she's in,' he said.

But the real reason he wanted to phone her was to prepare her for the awful reality that the dog she'd fallen in love with was about to be taken away from her.

GRETTA HAD SLEPT BADLY, but she couldn't blame Bertie. Tell a lie, she *could,* but only insofar as if she hadn't promised to look after him, she never would have met Jakob.

However, the blame for kissing him rested solely on her shoulders. Bertie couldn't be held responsible for *that.*

Looking back, she wasn't entirely sure who had made the first move: one moment he'd been walking towards the door and the next she'd been in his arms, his mouth on hers, and they'd been kissing.

Jakob had engulfed her. It was like being cuddled by an enormous teddy bear, and she'd allowed herself to relax into him for a moment, relishing the sensation. It had been such a very long time since she'd been held and she'd thoroughly enjoyed it.

For a second or two.

Until she'd realised what she was doing and had come to her senses. It pained her that Jakob had looked as mortified as she'd felt. He hadn't wanted it to happen, either. It had been as much of a shock to him.

They'd parted hurriedly. He hadn't been able to get away fast enough, and she'd desperately wanted him gone.

Shutting the door, she'd leant against it, her heart pounding, her stomach in knots, her emotions a jumbled, chaotic mess. She'd liked the kiss a lot. She liked *him*. Far too much. And she was scared.

All night she'd told herself that it was just a kiss. People kissed all the time.

Yeah, but not like that.

The passion that had swept through her for those few seconds had consumed her, and it had felt so good. So right.

Until common sense had smacked her on the forehead and demanded to know what the hell she was doing.

It's okay, she told herself. She didn't have to see him again. She could probably get Bertie's adoption sorted without involving Jakob. Maybe it could be done online, or via the main centre in Thornbury? She'd do it today, right now in fact, because although she was sitting at her desk, she wasn't doing any work. Concentration was beyond her this morning. She'd done little but stare at the screen for the past hour and think about Jakob. So she may as well get the adoption ball rolling.

Her phone was in her hand when it rang.

Letting out a squeak of surprise, she nearly dropped it. Then she saw Jakob's name on the screen and almost didn't answer.

Deciding to take the bull by the horns (because it had been her avoidance of confrontation that had allowed Landon to control her) she leapt in with, 'About yesterday—' but didn't get any further before Jakob cut her off.

'I've got Mr Butler's niece with me.'

'Pardon?' His words caught her unawares, and they didn't sink in straight away.

'Mr Butler's niece is here for Bertie.'

'But he's with me,' she replied stupidly, then realised what he was saying. Abruptly, she slumped back in her chair, the wind knocked out of her. 'Oh, I see.'

'I'm sorry.'

She could tell he was. He wasn't lying. But was he sorry for Bertie because the dog had bonded to her, or for her, because he knew how she felt about the little pooch?

Both, probably. He of all people, knew what it was like to love a dog. And she *did* love Bertie. In just a week he'd stolen her heart, and now she was about to be hurt once more.

So much for her vow of never allowing herself to fall in love again, but when she'd made it, she'd never imagined she'd lose her heart to *a dog*.

Gretta didn't hear most of what was said next, only that Jakob would be along shortly with Mr Butler's niece to collect Bertie and please could she have his things ready?

Numbly, she wandered around the house, dropping his toys, bowls, and blankets into a bag. Bertie, sensing something was up, followed her from room to room, his nose almost touching her leg as he whined anxiously.

It didn't take long to gather everything together. A matter of minutes. But she guessed it would be a long time before the pain of losing Bertie diminished.

This dog had left his paw prints on her heart.

IN THE YEARS THAT Jakob had worked at the sanctuary, he'd seen his fair share of distraught owners. If you loved an animal and had to give it up, for whatever reason, it was always distressing for everyone concerned. Especially the animals themselves, and try as he might, Jakob had never been able to harden his heart. It upset him every time.

Today was the worst.

'The dog is with his neighbour?' Erica seemed surprised after Jakob had told her who was looking after Bertie. 'The note said it had been brought here. If I'd known, I could have knocked on the door and saved you the trouble.' She stared at him brightly. 'I can do that anyway,' she added. 'No need to come with me.'

'I'm afraid there is,' he said. 'Bertie is in our care, so it's our responsibility to see him handed over.'

She shrugged. 'Okay, but will it take long? I've got a meeting with the solicitor at twelve-thirty.'

'It won't,' he assured her. 'There's some paperwork to sign first, then it's simply a matter of collecting him.'

But Jakob knew there wasn't going to be anything simple about it for Bertie or Gretta, and when he pulled up outside her

house, he felt like the biggest heel in the
world.

Gretta met them at the door, white-faced
and haunted-eyed.

She had Bertie in her arms.

The dog wriggled happily when he saw
Jakob, squirming and eager to get down
to give him a proper welcome. The
newcomer, his new rightful owner, he
ignored.

Burying her face in the dog's neck, Gretta
gave him a hug, holding onto him fiercely.
Then, without a word, she passed him to
Jakob. Her eyes glistened with unshed
tears and Jakob's jaw tensed.

He took a moment to give Bertie a cuddle
before gently putting him down. As Jakob
handed the lead to Erica, Bertie stood on
his back paws and scrabbled at Jakob's
legs, asking to be picked up again.

'So, you're Bertie, are you?' Erica said, leaning down. She hesitantly patted his head, and Bertie stopped pestering Jakob long enough to look at her.

Then he spied Zaza, who was sauntering down the hallway to see what was going on, and he lunged towards her, almost yanking the lead out of Erica's hand.

'My, he's stronger than he looks, isn't he?' She was eyeing him doubtfully,

'If you put him in your car, I'll bring his things,' Jakob offered.

'Lovely, thank you. As I said, I can't hang about.'

Two bags and the crate sat in the hall, and as he reached for them Gretta looked away, refusing to meet his gaze.

In a way, Jakob was glad, because he didn't think he could handle the pain he knew would be in her eyes. Saying goodbye to a dog was hard.

Yet Jakob realised that saying goodbye to Gretta was harder because, after this, he doubted he would see her again.

CHAPTER TWELVE

GRETTA HADN'T LEFT the house for two days. She'd had no reason to. There was no Bertie to walk, and she didn't need any groceries.

She'd assumed it would be easy to slip back into her old routine, that her week of looking after a dog would quickly become a distant memory, a blip in her otherwise sedate and serene life. But it hadn't worked like that. She *missed* him. The house that had once seemed so cosy, now felt cold. Her bed, without Bertie in it, was too big, too quiet, too *fragrant*. No chunky body snuggling into her, no snuffly snoring, no doggy whiffs. How daft was it to miss his smell, especially since she hadn't been too keen on waking up with a dog's nose on her pillow?

Even Zaza seemed to feel his absence. The day Mr Butler's niece had claimed him, the cat had paced from room to room like an old lady who couldn't remember where she'd left her glasses. And she'd been extra clingy and loving, too. Gretta felt judged, as though Zaza was scared that if *she* misbehaved, *she* might be handed over to a stranger on the doorstep.

For the hundredth (thousandth?) time, Gretta wondered how he was doing. Was he missing her? Had he settled in? Was Erica Hilliard making him sleep in the kitchen? Was she taking him on regular walks?

Each time one of those thoughts flitted through her head, Gretta would berate herself for being silly. Erica would be looking after him fine, and it probably would take him a few days to settle in. The poor little mite had been pushed from pillar to post recently, so he'd need time to realise that Erica was his new owner.

Gretta would need time too, and moping around the house wasn't helping. She should pop to the shops to pick up some artisan bread from the bakery and buy something nice for dinner. At least she didn't have to worry about Bertie howling the house down while she was out.

Telling herself that there surely must be more than *one* upside to not having Bertie in her life, she eased her feet into her trainers and grabbed a jacket. Then she had to bite her lip when she opened her mouth to call Bertie to her, momentarily forgetting that he was no longer there.

Maybe Jakob would have heard something? Would he have phoned or messaged Erica Hilliard to check up on the dog?

Thinking of Jakob gave her just as much of a pang as thinking of Bertie, and once again she cursed her stupidity. Kissing that man had been a big mistake. Thinking of him as being more than someone who worked at the animal sanctuary had been an even bigger one. She'd allowed him to slip under her defences, much like Bertie had slipped under the fence and escaped into Mr Butler's garden.

And now she was forced to recognise that she'd developed feelings for him.

So maybe, in a way, it was good that Bertie was no longer in her care? Without the dog, she'd have no reason to see or speak to Jakob.

But in the middle of the night, she could still feel his arms around her, his lips on hers. That kiss, no matter how fleeting it had been, had left a lasting impression on her body, just as the man himself had left a lasting impression on her mind.

Thank goodness it had only been a kiss, she thought, as she hurried along the street towards the shops, because the last thing she wanted was Jakob to have made a lasting impression on her *heart*.

The delicious aroma of warm, fresh bread filled her nose when she entered the bakers, and her mouth watered. Spoilt for choice and tempted by the goodies on display, she bought more than she needed, telling herself that she deserved a treat; and she was rather looking forward to soft cheese and tomato on sourdough, with a cream cake afterwards – until she glanced at the notices displayed in the post office's window and saw one announcing Mr Butler's funeral.

Oh, Bertie, she thought sadly, as a sudden longing for him swept through her.

She'd go, she decided. Pay her respects. And if the opportunity arose, she could ask after Bertie, make sure he was alright.

Now that her appetite had deserted her, Gretta decided against doing any more shopping, so she went home. Only to be struck with longing again once more as she realised how quiet her house was. Not even Zaza came to greet her: she was out, doing whatever feline things cats got up to when allowed to roam free.

Gretta put her shopping away, which took all of fifteen seconds, then climbed the stairs to her office. As always in times of stress or upset, work seemed like a good idea. But when she knocked her mouse and sent it tumbling to the floor, Gretta forgot about work as she scrabbled under the desk to retrieve it, and came face to face with one of Bertie's little stuffed animals.

Much to her dismay, her eyes filled with tears and she slumped against the side of the desk, holding the toy to her chest.

For the next half an hour she bawled her eyes out, crying both for Bertie and for herself – because she'd only just begun to come back to life, to start feeling again, *loving* again, only to have it snatched from her, plunging her back into the walled-up twilight world she'd been living in.

Gretta, it seemed, wasn't destined to live any other kind of life.

HOW WAS SHE? Jakob's fingers crept to the pocket of his jeans, as they'd done so many times during these past three days, and each time he'd changed his mind about calling her.

Gretta was fine. She'd only had the dog for just over a week, and the first few days hadn't counted because she'd hated every minute.

Jakob had no doubt that once the initial shock of handing Bertie over to his rightful owner had eased, Gretta's life would have gone back to the way it had been before a little French bulldog had turned it upside down. When she'd had a chance to think about it, she'd probably be glad of the lucky escape she'd had. No more poop picking, no more howling, no more muddy paw prints in her pristine house. Gretta was most definitely more suited to cat ownership than dog. And Zaza was probably glad to see the back of Bertie, as well. Both Gretta and the cat could return to their ordered lives without any more doggy disruption.

But was that strictly true? Jakob had seen her face when she'd given him up. She'd been distraught. So maybe she wasn't okay…?

He reached for his phone again, then stopped. Face-to-face would be better. He'd be able to see how she was doing for himself. It was so easy to lie over the phone or by message: 'I'm going to the gym after work', for instance…It was a lie he knew well, having been the perfect excuse for Clare to come home recently showered, and she'd certainly had a workout all right. Just not the kind Jakob had thought she'd been having. But when he'd confronted her, she hadn't been able to lie. Her mouth had said one thing, but her eyes had told a different story. *The truth.*

How was Gretta doing?

Jakob sighed; he couldn't seem to stop asking himself the question. He couldn't seem to get her out of his mind. It was because he felt responsible, he told himself. If it hadn't been for his blunt honesty when she'd phoned the day after she'd surrendered Bertie to The Forever Home to ask whether he was okay, Gretta wouldn't have felt guilty enough to take him back. And if she hadn't taken him back, she wouldn't have become attached to the pup.

Therefore, this whole situation was Jakob's fault.

He was to blame for both her upset and Bertie's.

As tempted as he was to contact Mr Butler's niece to ask, he knew he mustn't. Bertie was Erica's responsibility now: not his, or The Forever Home's, or Dawn's, or Gretta's. He just had to hope that the dog was being loved and cared for.

However, he could check on *Gretta*, and there was no time like the present since he'd finished his shift. He'd swing by on the way home. It would put his mind at rest and assuage his guilt.

As he drove down Muddypuddle Lane, he knew it wasn't just guilt he was feeling. It was also shame. He couldn't help thinking that he'd taken advantage of her the other evening. Although he honestly had no idea which of them had made the first move, he shouldn't have kissed her. She'd been upset and it had been wrong of him. Even if she hadn't been, he still shouldn't have done it. Aside from not being good boyfriend material, he didn't want a relationship. People let you down. Dogs didn't. He'd stick with dogs. They might break your heart when it was time for them to go over the rainbow bridge, but the love, loyalty and joy they brought was worth any amount of grief.

If Gretta only felt a fraction of that for Bertie, she'd be hurting right now, and he hated to think of her in pain.

The instant Jakob saw her face, he knew he'd been right to come, even though she'd been quick to cover her sadness.

'Hi.' Her tone was wary.

'I thought I'd...Are you...? I'm sorry I—'

Gretta leapt in before he could say anything further. 'No need to be. It's not like I haven't been kissed before.'

What?! Flustered he spluttered, 'That wasn't what I meant.' He could feel heat stealing into his cheeks and he hoped he wasn't blushing as much as he suspected he might be. Mortified and embarrassed, he explained, 'It's *my* fault you're upset over Bertie.'

Her expression was neutral, but from the glowing pink suffusing her skin, he assumed she was equally as embarrassed. She said, 'How do you work that out? I'm the one who promised to look after him.'

'I'm the one who persuaded you.'

She stared at him for longer than was comfortable, and he shifted self-consciously from foot to foot.

Then she said, 'I bought too many cakes this morning. Care to help me eat them?'

He nodded, relieved that the awkwardness had lifted. 'How's Zaza?' he asked, following her into the kitchen.

'Confused.'

'How are *you?*'

'I'm okay.' She had her back to him so he couldn't see her face, but her shoulders were rigid with tension.

'Look at me,' he said gently, and wasn't surprised to see tears in her eyes. 'You're not, are you?'

She bit her lip; her chin wobbled and he thought she was going to burst out crying, but she held it back. 'I will be. It's only a dog.'

Jakob gave her a look. She didn't mean that. Dogs were never *only* dogs. They were family, and Bertie had been part of hers, however briefly.

Gretta carried a plate of cream cakes into the sitting room and returned to the kitchen to finish making the drinks.

So that's all it had been, he thought, reflecting on what she'd just said – a kiss. Nothing more. What had he expected? Fireworks? The earth to move for her? At least he could rest easy now, knowing that she wasn't in the least bothered by it.

He was, though. She'd felt so incredibly good. She'd made *him* feel so incredibly good – until he'd come to his senses. Clearly, she hadn't been as affected as him.

'I'll get over it,' she said, and it took Jakob a second to realise that she was referring to Bertie. 'Mr Butler's funeral is on Thursday. I'm thinking of going.'

'Do you want some company?' he found himself asking, then tried to justify it by saying, 'I feel I ought to pay my respects because of Bertie.'

'It would be nice not to go on my own.' Gretta pulled a face. 'I miss the little guy. He really made himself at home, didn't he?'

'Would you have another dog?'

She shook her head. 'I doubt it. You get too attached to them, don't you?'

Jakob smiled sadly. 'That's kind of the point. It's unfortunate that you weren't able to adopt Bertie. If only Erica Hilliard had turned up a few days later...'

'I still don't think I could have kept him; it wouldn't have been right, morally. Bertie belongs with Mr Butler's family.'

'His niece wasn't even aware he had a dog,' Jakob pointed out. 'They couldn't have been close.'

'Neither were we. I feel I should have known more about him, since we were neighbours.' She looked so sad that his heart went out to her.

'Don't beat yourself up over it. You had your reasons.' And if he ever got his hands on that reason, he'd make the man that had caused her such pain sorry he'd been born.

Gretta studied him silently, and Jakob wondered what she was thinking, whether she was regretting telling him about her ex.

'About that kiss,' he blurted, cursing even as the words were leaving his lips. 'I'm not sorry at all.' Then, without giving her a chance to respond, he got to his feet and strode into the hall and out of the door, saying, 'See you Thursday.'

Thursday was three days away: plenty of time to reflect on what an idiot he was.

CHAPTER THIRTEEN

GRETTA WAS NERVOUS about seeing Jakob again. Combined with her worry over whether Bertie was okay and the fact that funerals were sad and sombre affairs, she wasn't looking forward to today.

There was a part of her that hadn't got the memo, however, and that was her heart, because it kept missing a beat every time she thought of Jakob – which was far too often and for far too long.

It was *his* fault. If he hadn't said what he'd said just before he'd left the other day, she'd have been able to put their kiss to the back of her mind. Pretend it had never happened. Ignore how it had made her feel. But he'd told her he wasn't sorry, then had left her alone for three days to reflect on what he'd meant.

Mind games – that had been her first instinct, her default setting; and no wonder after Landon. He'd been a master player. Jakob, though...? She didn't think so. Admittedly he could be abrupt and blunt sometimes, but not sly or mean, and he wasn't manipulative. He said what he meant, and not for effect or to provoke a reaction. So when he'd said he wasn't sorry he'd kissed her, he'd been telling the truth.

But what did it *mean?*

Gah! She was fed up thinking about it, but she couldn't stop, which was incredibly annoying because her mind was preoccupied with him when it should be concerned with more important things, like work, for instance.

So it was with trepidation that she heard the doorbell ring and went to answer it.

Jakob was wearing a suit.

Wow! Her eyes widened and her breath caught. He looked phenomenal: sexy, handsome, and totally at ease. A suit suited him.

'Ready?' he asked.

'Let me grab a jacket.' Gretta was wearing a smart, black knee-length dress and low heels. She'd felt overdressed until she'd seen Jakob. She hadn't known what to expect – jeans and a tee shirt, maybe? If that's what he'd turned up in, she wouldn't have cared; he was paying his respects, not taking part in a fashion show.

Not much was said on the drive to Thornbury until Gretta realised it was unlikely he'd come straight from work dressed like that. 'I could have met you at the church,' she pointed out. 'You needn't have picked me up. And you'll have to drive all the way back to Picklewick again to drop me off.'

'I wanted to, and I'll be going into work after the service,' he said, 'so I hope you don't mind if I call into mine on the way back, so I can get changed?'

Gretta didn't mind at all. She was curious to see where he lived. After all, she knew very little about him, just that he had two dogs (Trixie didn't count because he was fostering her) and his parents walked them for him while he was at work. It wasn't a lot, was it, considering he knew quite a bit about her?

He was as reticent and as private as she, and if he hadn't been there the day she thought she'd seen Landon walking down her street, she would never have told Jakob about him. And they wouldn't have kissed.

Did she regret it? She wasn't sure...

There was only a handful of people in the church when Gretta and Jakob arrived, and by unspoken agreement they sat in a pew a few rows back. Gretta recognised Miss Manning, the elderly woman she'd bumped into in the street the other day with Bertie, but the turn-out was distressingly small.

'I'm glad we came,' she said, leaning to whisper in Jakob's ear. He smelled of shampoo and soap. And himself. It was a smell that had lingered in her nose long after the kiss had ended— And she really *shouldn't* be thinking about that at a time like this.

'Me, too,' he replied, his voice low. 'There aren't many here, are there?'

'Bertie should have been here,' she said, a hitch in her voice. 'Mr Butler loved that dog, and the dog loved him.'

'Bertie wouldn't understand.'

'I know, but still...Is he okay, do you think?'

'I expect so.'

 Gretta's chin wobbled, and when Jakob glanced down at her, she pressed her lips together to hold back the sudden tears she didn't want him to see.

But he saw anyway because gently, hesitantly, he put his arm around her.

She stiffened, then slowly relaxed into him. Safe, that's what she felt, and cared for. He wasn't doing this for show or to exert any kind of pressure or control – he was doing this because she was in need of comfort.

Throughout the brief service, he kept his arm around her as she battled with her unexpected grief for a man she'd lived next door to for two years but had only spoken to when he'd been dying. She'd cut herself off so thoroughly from everyone and everything (apart from her cat) that she'd known nothing about the man whose funeral she was currently attending.

Ashamed, Gretta bowed her head and let her tears fall.

Jakob merely held her tighter.

When the coffin was carried out of the church, she followed it with her eyes and whispered, 'Bertie is okay, Mr Butler. He loves you and misses you, but he's okay.'

Her heart aching, she waited for the handful of the mourners to leave, then she and Jakob filed out behind them. There was some milling about as the coffin was loaded onto the hearse ready for its journey to the crematorium, and Gretta waited for an opportunity to speak to Erica.

'Thank you for coming,' the woman said. She looked tired and drawn.

'It was a lovely service,' Gretta replied. 'I wanted to pay my respects.' She glanced up at Jakob, who hadn't left her side. 'We both did. How is Bertie?'

Erica pressed her lips into a thin line. 'I don't know how my uncle put up with him. He's destroyed my favourite shoes and stole a loaf of bread off the table when my back was turned. You ought to have seen the mess. Oh, well, I dare say he'll settle down when he gets into a routine, which we should do now the funeral is over.' She heard her name being called. 'Sorry, the vicar wants me. Thanks again for coming.'

'That's that, then,' Gretta said sadly, as they left the churchyard.

'I don't feel like going back to work just yet,' Jakob said. 'There's a nice cafe around the corner – fancy a coffee?'

 Gretta didn't want to go home yet either, so a coffee sounded good.

'I would also suggest an early lunch, but my appetite's deserted me,' he said when they entered the cosy little cafe, and found a free table by the window.

'I don't think I could face anything either.'

'Will you be alright on your own?' he asked, then looked away, and she got the impression he felt awkward as he added, 'I mean, I'll have the dogs to take my mind off it, but when you work from home...'

'I'll be fine. Just a bit sad, that's all. Poor Mr Butler, I should have been a better neighbour.'

Jakob reached across the table and took her hand in his. 'You stepped up to the mark when he needed you. You took care of Bertie like he asked. Don't beat yourself up over it.'

Gretta gave him a small smile. He really *was* a nice guy, and she realised her sadness wasn't solely due to Mr Butler and Bertie – it was because this really would be the last time she'd see Jakob.

However, Jakob wasn't seeing *her* right now. He was gazing over her shoulder into the street, his expression stricken.

Gretta tried to see what had caught his attention, but there wasn't anything obvious. But when she turned back to him, his face was white, as though he'd seen a ghost.

I SHOULD EXPECT IT, Jakob told himself. *If you live in the same small town as your ex, you were bound to bump into them eventually.*

He hadn't 'bumped into her' as such, in that he was in the cafe and Clare was on the pavement outside, but their eyes met briefly and he knew she'd seen him. The contact had been too fleeting to gauge her reaction, and she was gone before he'd collected himself.

Distracted, he finished his coffee, then drove home to change out of his suit, leaving Gretta to wait for him in the car. He was desperate for a few moments alone, because the encounter with Clare had knocked the wind out of him. It was one thing glimpsing her in the distance; it was quite another being close enough to see that she hadn't changed a bit. If anything, she looked even more polished and glamorous than when she'd been his.

Ah, but she was never truly yours, was she? his sub-conscious piped up. She'd liked to share her love, and the fact that she'd worn his ring hadn't held her back.

It took him seconds to strip off his suit, shirt and tie, and change into his more usual attire of hiking trousers, walking boots and tee shirt, and he was back in the car in just over a minute.

'That was quick,' Gretta said.

'I told you I wouldn't be long.' He started the car and reversed off the drive.

'Thanks for coming with me, and for the coffee,' she said.

'It was my pleasure.' He blanched as he realised how that sounded. 'I didn't mean my *pleasure*. It was a funeral, not a—' He hunted around for a suitable word, but couldn't find one.

'I knew what you meant. Are you okay? You seem a little...' It was her turn to hesitate, and he guessed she didn't know how to describe his odd behaviour without being rude.

'Not too keen on funerals,' he said.

'Nor me. I'm glad it's over.'

He couldn't think of anything to say for the rest of the journey, so he didn't, and when he brought the car to a halt outside her house, all he could manage was, 'See you around.' Although, he highly doubted he would. Their paths hadn't crossed before Bertie, so there was no reason for them to cross now.

And that, more than anything that had happened today, made him feel incredibly sad.

'Did it go alright?' Maisie asked when he arrived at The Forever Home Kennels a short time later.

'As well as funerals go,' he replied. 'There weren't many there.'

'That's so sad.'

Yeah, 'sad' was the word of the day, he mused, as he checked on the work schedule and saw what still needed to be done.

It was whilst he was working out which of the dogs could be walked together, that he had the first of the three missed calls from Clare that he would receive over the next couple of hours.

When he saw her number come up, he sucked in a sharp breath, shock surging through him. He let the call go to voicemail, but when he checked a few seconds later, she hadn't left a message. Perhaps it hadn't been her? Perhaps he'd mis-remembered her number, and it had been someone else phoning him?

The second time the same number appeared on his screen, he didn't answer, but this time there *was* a message. 'Hi, it's me, Clare. Call me?'

Her voice sent a tremor down his spine.
The last time he'd heard it had been when
she'd told him she was leaving. But at
least he knew for certain that this number
was hers.

What could she want? To apologise? To
explain? To be *friends?*

Ha! As if that could ever happen. He
thought about blocking her, but he
couldn't bring himself to. Part of him
wanted to know why she was phoning
him, but another part, the self-
preservation part, thankfully wasn't
permitting him to phone her back.

Knowing her, she'd soon get the message
and give up. Or become distracted by
some other man.

That was it, Jakob surmised: she was
bored and at a loose end, so she thought
she'd see whether she could pick up where

she'd left off. He was under no illusion that if he let her back into his life, she'd soon be out of it again when she found someone else to amuse her.

He was once more debating whether to block her for his own sanity, when he had yet another call, quickly followed by a message.

Can we talk?

This time he did block her because he was scared he might be weak enough to let her back into his life – and terrified he might discover he still loved her after all.

GRETTA EMAILED THE final book blogger and sat back. Another job ticked off her to-do list, but there were plenty more left.

She'd take a break, have something to eat and stretch her legs, then—

Where would she stretch her legs *to?* A walk around the block without a canine companion to accompany her seemed odd.

Just something to eat then, although she didn't know what. She hadn't had much of an appetite since Bertie left, and the funeral earlier today had killed off what little remained.

Appalled, Gretta closed her eyes: bad turn of phrase.

But it was true, she hadn't felt like eating. It was now gone six in the evening though, and whether she felt like it or not, she should have something. Anyway, Zaza would be demanding to be fed soon. Bertie's absence hadn't affected *the cat's* appetite.

Gretta made her way downstairs, her back and hips stiff from sitting at her desk for so long. As she opened the fridge and closed it again, her mind was on Jakob. Something had upset him in the cafe earlier, but he'd brushed it off. She could tell though, because his whole demeanour had changed in an instant. He'd closed up, tension apparent in his hunched shoulders, rigid jaw, and white-knuckled grip on his coffee mug. He'd not said much afterwards, replying to her in monosyllables, his thoughts clearly elsewhere. Was he worried?

Gretta wasn't sure, but Jakob hadn't been the same man he'd been a minute earlier.

She'd sat in his car, waiting for him to get changed, and wracked her brains. Had it been something she'd said or done? She didn't think so...But whatever it was, he hadn't wanted to talk about it, and he'd been keen to take her home.

Gretta was concerned by how much that hurt.

The sound of her doorbell ringing made her freeze, but only for an instant. There was only *one person* it could be! Her heart thumping, a smile spreading across her face, she hurried to answer it.

Yanking the door open, she said, 'Jakob—' Then stopped.

Taylor was standing there; a visibly pregnant Taylor, and she was holding a large bunch of orange roses and apricot-tinted gerbera.

'What are you doing here?' Gretta knew she was being blunt and unfriendly (un*sister*ly), but the words tumbled out as disappointment set in.

'Can I come in?'

Gretta glanced up and down the street, then stood to the side.

'These are for you.' Taylor thrust the bouquet at her.

'You're pregnant.'

'I know.' Her sister's expression became wry as she stroked her bump.

Numb, Gretta showed her into the living room. 'How long? I mean, how—?'

'How far along? Twenty-six weeks.'

'That's...' Gretta tried to work it out in her head, but she couldn't get her brain to function. The last person she'd expected to see was *Taylor*.

'Six months.'

'Bloody hell, Taylor! You could have told me on the phone.'

'I'm not here because I'm pregnant, although I thought you should know since you're going to be their aunt.'

Floored, Gretta sank onto the arm of a chair.

'Do you mind if I sit down?' Taylor asked, somewhat sharply.

'God, no, please do. Is there anything I can get you? Water?'

'The flowers are from Mum.'

'Oh, right. Tell her thanks.'

'You should tell her yourself. What's going on with you, Gretta? Don't you think you've been a cow for long enough?'

'*What?*' Gretta's mouth dropped open. '*Me?* I'm not a cow.'

'You certainly act like one. Ever since you and Landon got together, you thought you were too good for us. You never visited our parents or me. You never invited us to yours; hell, you couldn't even be bothered to phone! Then you walk out on Landon, and no one hears from you for weeks, months even. It nearly destroyed him. If it was up to me, I'd let you rot, but it's killing Mum and Dad. They're worried sick about you.'

At the words 'it nearly destroyed him', Gretta began to laugh. It was high pitched and rather manic, and she couldn't seem to stop.

Taylor stared at her in disbelief, her mouth agape. 'What the hell is so funny?'

'Landon,' Gretta gasped, wiping her eyes. She was uncertain whether they were tears of laughter or pain. '*He* nearly destroyed *me*. And *you*—' she hitched in a breath, the tears definitely from pain now

'—didn't even notice. None of you did! You never have. Miss Invisible, that's me. Bolshy Taylor, flighty Sierra, and invisible Gretta.'

'Oh, grow up, Gretta. You've never been invisible. You were Miss Goody-Two-Shoes, the perfect daughter. Do you know how many times Mum held you up as a paragon of daughterly behaviour when me or Sienna went off the rails?'

'She did not!'

'She *did*. I can't believe you didn't notice. Or is all this an excuse for behaving like a—?'

'It's not an excuse! If I was such a *'paragon of daughterly behaviour'* how come none of you noticed what Landon was doing to me?' Gretta screeched.

Taylor froze, then she began shaking her head as Gretta's words sank in. 'Please don't tell me he hurt you. Please don't say that.' She looked distraught, and the shock and dismay on her face was enough to calm Gretta a little.

'He didn't hurt me physically,' she explained, wiping her face with her sleeve. 'It was emotional abuse. Landon wrote the book on gaslighting.'

Something seemed to click into place for Taylor. 'You've got a *cat.*'

'Yes.'

'You didn't have one before because *Landon* didn't like them?'

'Yes. I told you that on the phone.'

'You did, but I didn't realise what you meant. *Oh, Gretta,* why didn't you tell us?'

Gretta's voice was small as she said, 'I was invisible, remember?'

'*No, you weren't.* Look at me Gretta, you've *never* been invisible. You were sensible and conscientious, a bit of a goody-two-shoes, but that's what we love about you.' There were tears streaming down her cheeks. 'Please tell Mum and Dad what you've told me.'

'I've hurt them,' Gretta realised. She also realised something else: that she was still allowing Landon to control her. She'd thought she was free of him, but by running away and hiding from the world she hadn't been free of him at all – she'd been doing *exactly* what he'd programmed her to do.

Was she free of him now? Now that everything was out in the open? Did he really have any more power over her?

She thought not. She was done with hiding away, done with thinking that she wasn't worthy of being loved. It was time she started living again.

And maybe time to start loving again, too...

CHAPTER FOURTEEN

IT HAD BEEN AN emotional couple of weeks, Gretta acknowledged, beginning with discovering Mr Butler collapsed on the floor and ending with hugs and tears with her family.

She'd felt wrung out for a while after confiding to Taylor how awful her relationship with Landon had been, followed by having to explain it all again to her mum and dad. Her dad, bless him, had threatened to dig out his old boxing gloves and 'teach Landon a lesson he wouldn't forget' and had had to be restrained by her mum, but eventually they'd all agreed that Gretta should put it behind her and concentrate on the future.

So that's what she was trying to do.

She'd already made a good start in that she had a place of her own in Picklewick and a job she enjoyed (although her father wasn't entirely convinced that being a virtual assistant was a 'proper' job). Admittedly, she didn't have a social life, and a romantic relationship wasn't on the cards yet, but—

Or was it? she wondered, as yet another image of Jakob flashed across her mind.

She kept thinking about him, wondering how he was, what he was doing. And she also kept thinking about that kiss, and his declaration that he hadn't been sorry. Then there was his strange behaviour on the day of Mr Butler's funeral, and she wished she knew what had spooked him.

Although she'd not known him long, Gretta missed him. She was also still missing Bertie, and she couldn't believe how much of an impact the dog had made on her life in such a short time. She'd hoped (assumed) that she'd get used to not having him around, but if anything, she felt his absence more keenly than ever. And with each passing day, the thought of fostering a dog became more appealing.

She'd been able to give Bertie a loving home for the short time she'd had him, so why couldn't she open her home to another dog in desperate need, especially since she now had a bit more experience. And Jakob. She could always ask Jakob for advice.

There was one thing she needed to be sure of, though – that she would be doing this for the dogs and not for herself, that she wasn't doing it so that she'd see more of Jakob.

If she took him out of the equation, would she still be as keen to foster?

When she arrived at the conclusion that she would, she knew what she had to do. She'd sleep on it tonight and if she still felt the same in the morning, she'd pay The Forever Home on Muddypuddle Lane a visit.

DESPITE KNOWING THAT Clare couldn't contact him now that he'd blocked her, Jakob had been on pins since the day of Mr Butler's funeral. And because he didn't want to risk bumping into her, he stayed away from Thornbury's town centre or the supermarket, preferring to drop into

Picklewick on the way home from work if he needed anything.

He also secretly hoped he might spot Gretta on the high street, but he'd not even caught a fleeting glimpse. Mind you, he probably wasn't in the best frame of mind to see her again. Clare being back on the scene, had reopened old wounds and brought long-buried emotions to the surface.

He liked Gretta enormously, and he fancied her even more, but he was too scared to take it further.

Jakob was in the middle of hosing down the patio at the rear of his bungalow when he paused, his arm dropping to his side, water cascading over his boots. Stan whined, his tail waving as he gave Jakob a pleading look. The retriever adored water and loved nothing more than to launch himself repeatedly through the spray. Ripley barked at it, as though the hosepipe was an incredibly long and dangerous snake that spat water, while Trixie sat on the wooden bench, keeping her paws dry as she watched the proceedings.

The little dog had come a long way since Jakob had started fostering her and was now happier and more confident. He'd miss her when she found her forever home.

But he'd paused, not because Trixie would leave him one day, but because it suddenly struck him that he was lonely. He loved his dogs with all his heart and then some, and he could never imagine being without a canine companion in his life; however, since he'd met Gretta, he'd found himself enjoying her company more and more. And now that she was no longer around, he'd come to realise just how much. But was he feeling lonely enough to launch himself into another relationship?

Opening his heart again was risky, fraught with danger, and even now, he feared he might still have feelings for Clare. If she hadn't returned to Thornbury maybe he would have had the courage to ask Gretta out. But Clare had, and until he was clear in his mind that he was over her, he couldn't contemplate being with anyone else. Not even someone as lovely as Gretta. Especially since she hadn't seemed as moved by their kiss as he'd been.

A boop on his leg from Stan reminded him that he was supposed to be cleaning up his backyard, although the cleaning had mostly all been done, and it was now playtime for the pooches, so he began spraying water around again.

The dogs heard his visitor arrive before he did. Their body language alerted him. Both dogs had frozen, staring towards the side gate, their ears pricked, their heads cocked. Even Trixie was on alert, and when the sound of someone knocking on the front door reached them, all three sprang into action, dashing to the back door hoping to be allowed in to greet whoever it was. They knew better than to bark, but a visitor always caused a kerfuffle.

Jakob wasn't expecting anyone, and he knew his parents were busy today so it couldn't possibly be them. It was probably a delivery driver with a parcel for a neighbour, chancing his arm that someone could take it in. Jakob didn't usually mind, but his boots were wet, as were the dog's paws, and he didn't want water tracked through the house, so he went to the side gate instead and peered through it.

A car he didn't recognise was parked on the road, partially blocking his drive.

With a sigh, he thought he should go see who it was, and his hand was on the latch when he heard a woman call, 'Jakob? Are you there?'

His stomach dropped. He knew that voice.

It was *Clare*.

She knocked again, rattling the letterbox, and slowly, quietly, he backed away from the gate, then clicked his fingers and gestured for the dogs to come to heel.

Stan obeyed immediately, but Ripley took another click before he did as he was told. Trixie just looked flummoxed.

Jakob shrank against the wall, despite knowing that Clare couldn't possibly see him, and waited with bated breath, praying she would leave before one of the dogs gave him away.

When she finally went, he let out a shaky sigh and unpeeled himself from the wall, his heart thudding.

He was going to have to speak to her eventually, he realised, but not yet. He didn't think he could face her just yet.

THE FOLLOWING MORNING Gretta felt the same as she had yesterday. She hadn't changed her mind: she still wanted to foster a dog. So she showered, got dressed (taking a little more care with her appearance than usual) and headed out the door.

She wasn't expecting to bring a dog home with her today, but if she could start the ball rolling (she wasn't entirely sure what that would entail) it would be something.

The morning was warm for the time of year, with blue skies and fluffy clouds. It felt good to be out, even if she was in the car. It would have been a perfect day to take a dog for a walk, if only she had one.

Feeling hopeful that the situation would be rectified soon (although she had a feeling no dog could replace Bertie in her heart) Gretta felt happier than she had in a while.

It had taken her longer than it should have done to get to this point after she'd walked out on Landon, but she was here now, and as far as she was concerned things could only get better. She'd reconciled with her family, and now realised that she *was* loved and valued, she had her own home, a job she loved, a gorgeous cat (*up yours, Landon!*), and she was about to see a man who was beginning to mean a lot to her.

Hang on, shouldn't that last bit be *about to foster a dog*? Because that *was* the reason she was trundling up Muddypuddle Lane right now, wasn't it? *Okay, one* of the reasons. The *main* reason, obviously. It would be a bonus if she got to see Jakob. Hopefully it wasn't his day off. Or he wasn't out walking a dog, or taking one to the vet, or...

Let's face it, she said to herself, she was going to be seriously disappointed if he wasn't there.

To her delight, when she drove onto the gravelled area, she saw his car, and her anticipation rose.

She parked up and got out, wondering whether to go looking for him, before deciding it might be rude. She ought to make her presence known at the office, like she'd done last time when she'd had Bertie with her.

A pang shot through her as she thought of the little dog and how she'd left him here. He'd been so miserable...

Gretta walked over to the office, various canine voices filling the air, and as she went inside she couldn't help musing that one of them might belong to a pooch who would come to stay with her for a while. A small dog, preferably, but then she recalled how gentle Jakob's golden retriever was and she decided to keep an open mind. Besides, Jakob wouldn't let her have a dog she couldn't cope with. She had complete trust that he'd do right by her and the dog.

Trust. There was that word again. She trusted him, and it was a nice feeling.

'Hiya,' Maisie said, catching sight of her in the cramped reception area. 'It's Gretta, isn't it? Bertie, the French bulldog?'

Gretta was surprised she remembered. 'That's right.'

'Jakob told me all about you, how you took Bertie in. You're a star!'

She was? 'Is Jakob around? I wanted a quick word. I miss Bertie a lot, and although I'm not ready for another dog, I thought maybe I could foster one?'

'He's on the phone to Dawn in Thornbury. Can you give him five minutes?'

'Of course.'

'Tell you what, would you like to sniff some puppies while you wait?'

'Excuse *me?*'

'Sniff puppies. They've got the most gorgeous milky smell. There's a litter in the house, and I was about to give them their first taste of solid food. Would you like to give me a hand?'

'Ooh, yes, please! *Puppies!*'

'I know, right? Aside from kittens, there's nothing cuter.' Maisie left the office, still talking, as Gretta hastily followed.

Maisie chattered, 'They're just over three weeks old. Little round blobs of cuteness, with four tiny paws, a tail, and the most adorable little noses. Their mother was brought in heavily pregnant – an accidental litter. Her owners couldn't afford to get her spayed, and one day she got out. Two months later, they realised she was going to have puppies.'

Maisie led her into an old farmhouse that looked as though it had recently been renovated.

'Mum and pups are in the utility room,' she said. 'I haven't been able to get to my washing machine for weeks! But it's the most secure place for them. Here they are!'

She stepped aside so Gretta could get a look.

Gretta stifled a squeal and put a hand to her mouth because, lying in a wooden box lined with towels, was a small grey dog and six tiny puppies.

'Oh, my God,' she breathed. 'They're so little.'

'You should have seen them when they were born! They've doubled in size since then.' Maisie crouched on the floor, patted and stroked the mother dog, then picked up one of the pups. 'Here you go,' she said, and handed it to Gretta.

She took it gingerly, terrified she was going to hurt it.

'Don't be scared,' Maisie said. 'They're more robust than you think, and it's crucial for their development that they get used to being handled. Have a sniff – I dare you.'

Gretta brought the puppy to her face, the little body warm and squirmy, and inhaled. 'Oh, my...'

'See! I told you. I wish I could bottle that smell.'

The puppy licked Gretta's nose, and she giggled.

Maisie said, 'I'm just going to mix up some puppy food with milk – milk suitable for dogs, that is – so will you be okay here for a minute?'

She most certainly would! She'd happily stay here all day, she thought, as she held the soft, furry pup close, and listened to its tiny squeaky whimpers.

No wonder Jakob loved his job so much if he got to cuddle puppies!

Gretta hoped he wouldn't finish doing whatever he was doing too soon, because even though she dearly wanted to see him, she was having far too much fun playing with six adorable pups.

'WHAT THE HELL?' Jakob muttered when he saw who was standing at the end of the row of pens. What was *she* doing here?

He narrowed his eyes.

Clare smiled brightly back. 'It's me,' she said unnecessarily, and gave a kind of shrug.

'So it is.'

'Don't be like that, Jakey.'

'I'm not being like anything,' he told her.

She sauntered towards him, her hips swinging.

Jakob swallowed nervously. 'What do you want?'

'To talk to you.'

'Now is not a good time.' He didn't think *any* time would be good. 'I'm busy. Working. I'm at work.'

'I know.' Her gaze swept briskly around the kennels. There was no warmth in her eyes, no acknowledgement of the plight of the poor dogs. 'You didn't call, you didn't reply to my messages. I even went to your house yesterday. No joy. Are you avoiding me, Jake?'

'I don't see that we've got anything to talk about,' he replied, wishing she wouldn't call him Jake. No one else did. Just her.

She hung her head, her long blond hair falling like a curtain to hide her face. 'I'm sorry, Jake. I was stupid.'

Nuh-uh, *he* had been the stupid one, for taking her back after the first time. And the second. And the third.

'I made a mistake,' she continued.

Yeah, she could say that again.

'Aren't you going to say anything?' She was peeping up at him from under her lashes and twirling her hair around her finger. It was her flirting pose.

'There's nothing to say.'

'I'm *sorry*,' she repeated. 'I wish I could turn the clock back, but I can't. I wish I'd realised...' She trailed off and stepped closer.

Jakob held his ground. He didn't want her to think she intimidated him.

As he gazed down at her, she took another step, lifted her chin and looked into his eyes. 'I didn't want to hurt you. It's just...I wanted more excitement. But I realise now that excitement isn't everything. Love is more important, and you really did love me, didn't you, Jake?'

Jakob fought to keep his expression neutral. He *had* loved her, with every fibre of his being and then some. But as he studied her, he finally realised something – *he didn't love her anymore.* Each time she'd been unfaithful, some of that love had eroded away. That last, awful affair had swept it away like a tsunami, but in the raging torrent of his grief, he hadn't realised.

Abruptly he was glad she'd come back, glad that she'd tracked him down, glad they'd had this talk. Because he could put his hand on his heart and say he no longer loved her.

'I think you still do,' she murmured. She was so close he could feel the warmth of her skin and smell her perfume, the same fragrance she always used to wear. The scent had no effect on him, neither did her body, which she abruptly pressed against him as she reached up to wind her arms around his neck.

And when she tried to kiss him, he felt nothing. *Absolutely nothing.*

With relief, Jakob knew he was finally, irrevocably, free of her.

BUBBLING WITH EXCITEMENT and an overload of furry cuteness, Gretta hurried towards the block of kennels where the sanctuary dogs were housed. She'd spent longer than she'd intended with the puppies, and even now she'd had to drag herself away. She couldn't wait to see Jakob and tell him what she'd been doing.

If she was honest, she couldn't wait to see him *full stop*.

Gretta rounded a corner and skidded to a halt.

She could see him alright.

And she wished she couldn't, because some woman was draped all over him. No, not *some woman*, Gretta realised in dismay. It was the woman from the supermarket a couple of weeks ago. The one who someone called Jake had adored.

Jake...Jakob...? *Oh, hell.*

A sharp pain struck her in the chest, and she staggered back, then turned on her heel and stumbled away.

That would teach her to trust a man. She should have known better. She *did* know better.

Unfortunately, she'd allowed herself to hope.

Her heart aching, tears in her eyes, Gretta vowed she would never, *ever* make that mistake again.

JAKOB EXPERIENCED a certain satisfaction on seeing the disbelief on Clare's face as she pulled away when he refused to respond.

As she'd tried her best to kiss him, he'd stood there, immobile and resolute, waiting for the realisation that she couldn't talk him around this time, to sink in.

When it did, she didn't look happy. Her eyes were flinty, and her lips were pressed into a thin line. But not for long, because she soon had something to say about his lack of response.

'She's a bit mousy, isn't she?' Clare spat.

Jakob lifted his chin. He might have known: it was okay for *her* to mess about, then bugger off with his best mate, but she now had the cheek to feel hard-done-by because he'd moved on. Or she *thought* he had, because she'd seen him holding Gretta's hand in the cafe on the day of Mr Butler's funeral.

Was that what had brought her to his door, so to speak? A dog-in-the-manger attitude?

She hadn't wanted him, but even after three years, she didn't want anyone else to have him. Or – and this was also a possibility – she assumed she'd snap her fingers, and he'd come running, dumping Gretta in the process.

Gretta was worth ten of Clare. A hundred. She was genuine, kind, loving and he wanted her so badly.

One kiss would never be enough...

'Go away, Clare,' he said with a weary sigh. 'I'm not interested. I haven't been interested for a very long time.' Then he turned his back on her and waited for her to leave.

It took a few seconds, but eventually he heard her march away, and only when her footsteps had faded entirely did he allow himself to relax. He was free of her. It was time to start living his life again, and maybe, if he was lucky, he could allow himself to *love* again.

And when Gretta's face swam into his mind, he smiled.

CHAPTER FIFTEEN

ONE STEP FORWARD, one step back. That's how Gretta felt right now, as she took her seat at her desk. Just as she thought she might be able to open her heart to another man, that man had proved to be a big disappointment.

She'd returned from The Forever Home yesterday feeling betrayed and upset, and extremely jealous, but had managed to talk some sense into herself overnight.

She and Jakob had kissed.

So what? It had hardly been a declaration of love and, as she thought back to the conversation she'd inadvertently overheard in the supermarket that day, Clare (that was the woman's name) and Jakob had history. *A lot* of history.

According to her friend, he used to worship the ground Clare walked on. *Adored her –* wasn't that what she'd said? He clearly still loved her if they were now back together, and Gretta couldn't begrudge him that. She hoped he'd be happy.

But she wasn't quite ready to see him again, so perhaps she'd shelve her dog fostering plans for a while. She'd get her life back on an even keel first, then see if she felt the same. To be honest, she thought she probably would, because she still missed Bertie. Every now and then she swore she heard the click of his claws on the tiles in the kitchen, or felt a boop on her leg. She even imagined she could hear him howling, that *Aaawooohooo* which tugged at her heartstrings and—

The ringing of the doorbell broke through her thoughts and with a sigh she rose to answer it.

She was only halfway down the stairs when whoever was outside began hammering on the door.

'I'm coming!' she shouted, worry pricking at her.

It swiftly turned to incredulity when she saw Harriet Brown and Bertie on the pavement.

'What—?' she began, but didn't get any further as the dog launched himself at her legs. She staggered back, Bertie leaping up, uttering cries of joy. 'Bertie? What are—?'

'I'm calling the police,' Harriet snapped. 'My husband works nights and he needs his rest. He can't be expected to sleep with that racket going on. And why is the dog out on the street on his own, that's what I want to know!'

So did Gretta. She knelt, cuddling Bertie, who wriggled and squirmed ecstatically, trying to lick her face.

'You shouldn't have a dog if you can't look after it,' Harriet carried on.

'He's not mine. He belongs to Mr Butler's niece. She came to fetch him a couple of weeks ago.'

That took the wind out of the woman's sails somewhat. 'I thought I hadn't seen it around recently,' she sniffed. 'You need to get her to come and fetch it. And tell her to take better care of it in future.'

'I will,' Gretta promised, hugging him. God, she'd missed him so much. He had to go back to his rightful owner, though, no matter how dearly she wanted to keep him. The problem was, she realised, as she took him inside, she didn't have any contact details for Erica Hilliard.

Jakob undoubtedly would, but Gretta didn't feel up to speaking with him. She'd give the sanctuary in Thornbury a call. They'd surely know.

She was tempted to leave it an hour or so, revelling in having Bertie back, even if it was temporary, but she guessed Erica would be going frantic with worry. So, with a heavy heart, she called the animal sanctuary and explained the situation.

'I'll just put you through to someone who can help,' the person on the other end said, putting her on hold.

To Gretta's dismay, the 'someone' she was put through to was Jakob.

'Gretta, hi.' He sounded happy. She guessed she knew the reason for that.

'Bertie's turned up on my doorstep,' she said, without preamble.

There was a pause before he said, 'I see. Shall I come and collect him?'

'If you give me Erica Hilliard's address, I'll take him back there myself.'

He hesitated again, and when he said, 'Sorry, I can't give out personal information,' she realised he was right. 'I can call her and ask if she minds,' he offered, and she had to be content with that.

When he phoned back with Erica's address a short while later, she gave a sigh of relief that she wouldn't have to see him.

Or was it disappointment? She honestly couldn't say; but either way, it was for the best. Jakob's heart belonged to someone else, and she simply had to accept it.

ERICA HILLIARD LIVED on a busy street on the other side of Thornbury, in a terraced Victorian house set in the middle of a row of similar houses. She had a small front garden, laid to slab and sporting a selection of pots, which was separated from the pavement by a wrought-iron gate, and there were net curtains at the windows. When Gretta pulled up alongside, she saw Erica peering through them.

The door opened before Gretta reached it. She was carrying Bertie because she didn't have a lead or a harness, and she swore she felt him deflate when he realised where he was. He sagged in her arms like a cuddly toy with its stuffing removed.

Before she had time to consider what that meant, Erica hurried outside, a frown on her face.

'The little sod!' she cried. 'I can't believe he made it all the way to Picklewick.'

Gretta also found that hard to believe. Thornbury was nine miles from Picklewick. It was quite a distance for little legs, and there were so many dangers along the way. The thought of all the vehicles he must have passed, filled her with horror.

'Check your garden,' Gretta advised, handing him over reluctantly. Her arms immediately felt empty. She wanted to snatch him back and take him home.

The woman sighed. 'I have. This is the third time he's escaped. I've got three kids and two grandkids, and he's caused me more worry than all of them put together. I don't know what I'm going to do with him. He's more trouble than he's worth. If he carries on behaving like this, I'm going to take him to The Forever Home Kennels, and hope your boyfriend can find someone to give him a home. In fact, I should have told him that when he phoned me. You could have taken the little sod straight there – it would have saved me the bother.'

'He's not my boyfriend.'

'What?' Erica was distracted. 'You were at the funeral together, so I assumed—'

'*I'll* take Bertie,' Gretta blurted.

The woman blinked, hoisting the dog onto her hip and grimacing. 'I've got to put him down. He's getting heavy.'

'I'll take him,' Gretta repeated.

'What do you mean 'take him'? Back to the kennels?'

'No, I'll take him off your hands. He can live with me. I'll be his new owner. If you're serious?'

'Oh, I'm serious. I've got enough on my plate without him.'

Gretta held out her arms.

Erica stared at her suspiciously. 'You won't try to bring him back if he plays you up?'

'I won't, I promise. I'll give him a good home.'

Erica didn't move, and Gretta feared the woman was going to refuse her offer. *Please let me have him*, she begged silently. It was clear that Erica didn't care for the dog and Bertie wasn't happy living with Erica. He looked dejected and defeated, and Gretta could see that he was shutting down – just like Jakob had said he'd done in the kennel.

She couldn't let that happen.

Erica made up her mind. 'Here, have him.' She dumped Bertie into Gretta's waiting arms and Gretta staggered at the weight. 'He's your responsibility now – is that clear?'

'Perfectly.'

'Good. Wait there, I'll get his basket and stuff.'

She disappeared inside and Gretta whispered in Bertie's ear, 'Don't worry, I won't make you sleep in it.'

The dog squirmed, reaching up to flick her on the nose with his sloppy pink tongue.

Gretta popped him in the car, and Erica returned a minute later holding a plastic dog bed. In it were a couple of bowls, some toys, three tins of cheap dog food, and his lead and harness.

'Sorry about the manky cardigan in the bottom, but he seems to like sleeping on it,' she said. 'I threw it out once, but he knocked the bin over and dragged it back out. You wouldn't believe the mess he made. There was rubbish all over my kitchen floor.'

Gretta smiled. She definitely *would* believe it: she'd had first-hand experience, and she'd been equally appalled.

'Are you sure about this?' she checked, remembering that she hadn't fallen in love with him instantly. It had taken her losing him to realise exactly what she'd lost.

Unbidden, Jakob leapt into her mind and she pushed him away. She'd never had him, therefore she'd never lost him, but she was realising how much she'd grown to care for him and how much she missed his company – the kiss aside.

'I'm sure. He's too much work. I haven't got the time or the patience for a pet.'

Bertie is so much more than a pet, though, Gretta objected silently as she drove back to Picklewick with the dog on the back seat. He'd worked his way into her heart and was there to stay.

GRETTA HAD HOPED to have a better night's sleep now that her warm and chunky companion was cuddled next to her and Zaza on the bed, but she didn't.

Cross and feeling unaccountably lonely, she gave up trying to sleep at around two a.m. and padded downstairs to make a mug of cocoa. Taking it back to bed with her, she decided that if the hot, soothing drink didn't have the desired effect, she'd get up for good and start her day.

With the soft glow of the bedside lamp illuminating the room, Gretta sipped her cocoa and tried not to think about things she'd rather not think about. However, as so often happened in the depths of the night before dawn had yet to smudge the horizon, when she switched off the light and settled down again, that was all she could think about.

At least her thoughts hadn't centred on Landon for once, which was a relief. Instead, she kept thinking about Jakob and the kiss. Then Jakob and the woman from the supermarket.

'Oh, Jakob,' she murmured sadly.

As though sensing her unhappiness, Bertie wriggled up the bed until his nose was touching her shoulder. He whined, and she fondled his silky ears. 'I know you liked him, but we won't be seeing him again,' she said sorrowfully. 'He's got a girlfriend, so it's just you, me and Zaza from now on.' Stroking his soft fur, she added, 'It's probably a good thing that he does. I don't think I'm ready to let another man into my life. Except you.' She kissed his nose. 'You're different.'

He snuggled in closer, burying his face in her neck.

'I'm so glad you're back, Bertie,' she said, her eyes welling with tears. 'We don't need him, do we? *I* don't need him, not when I've got you and Zaza.' She had her parents and her sisters now, too: she'd be okay.

But as she finally drifted off to sleep, Gretta deliberately ignored the little voice in her head asking whether *okay* was really the best she could hope for.

CHAPTER SIXTEEN

FRITZ WAS AN ENERGETIC Border collie who needed a lot of exercise to keep him well and happy: something his former owners hadn't realised when they'd bought him as a puppy. Now two years old, he was full of life and energy, needing to be kept physically and mentally active, and today Jakob had set himself the task of wearing him out.

However, after traipsing around the hills and moorland above Picklewick for two hours and several miles, Jakob realised *he* was the one who was worn out, not the dog. Fritz was as lively and as alert as when they'd set off. The same could not be said for him.

It didn't help that he hadn't slept well last night. He'd been awake for half of it, thinking about Gretta and Bertie, worrying that they were both alright. When he'd spoken to her yesterday, he'd been shocked that Bertie had found his way back to Picklewick, uplifted to hear her voice again, then crushed that she hadn't wanted him to accompany her when she'd taken the dog back to Erica. She'd been distant and reserved, just as she'd been the first few times they'd met. Had he imagined the thaw? Had it been wishful thinking on his part because he liked her so much? Had Bertie been the only connection between them?

Jakob refused to believe it. There had definitely been a spark, which had ignited into a flame when they'd kissed. Surely it couldn't have been so easily extinguished?

While he was wondering whether he should call her or send her a message (although he had no idea what to say), Jakob saw a flash of black and white on the path leading from the village to Muddypuddle Lane.

He slowed his pace, squinting, convinced it was a dog. Fritz had seen it too: his ears were pricked, his head was up, and he was on full alert.

Jakob came to a stop in the middle of the lane and used his hand to shade his eyes.

'Bertie!' The dog's name tore from his lips. 'What the hell?'

Bertie heard his name and bounced to a halt, casting around to find where the call had come from.

'Bertie!' Jakob shouted again, and the dog zeroed in on his voice, racing towards him, barking excitedly.

But for all Bertie's happiness on seeing him, signified by stumpy tail wagging and excited whimpering, the little chap was clearly exhausted. His tongue was hanging out, and once the initial greeting was over, he flopped onto his tummy, his back legs splayed behind him.

'What are you doing up here, boy?' Jakob asked, checking him over. He seemed okay, despite having made the trip from Thornbury to Picklewick twice in as many days. In fact, he was in remarkably good condition, considering.

Scooping Bertie up, Jakob tucked him into the crook of his arm. He'd put Fritz in his kennel and settle him in, then he'd take Bertie back to Erica Hilliard. And while he was there, he'd have a word with the woman about taking better care of her dog and offer her some advice on how to keep him secure and stop him escaping.

Jakob had to take his hat off to the pup, though. Bertie was determined. And resourceful.

Maybe he thought he'd have more luck with Jakob than he'd had with Gretta and be allowed to stay?

It broke Jakob's heart to think the dog wasn't happy and was pining for Picklewick, but unfortunately Jakob had to return him.

As he bundled him into the crate in the back of his car, it briefly crossed Jakob's mind to phone Gretta and let her know that Bertie had escaped again, but if he did, it would be just an excuse to talk to her, so instead he dialled Erica's number.

'Erica? It's Jakob from Thornbury Animal Sanctuary. I'm at The Forever Home Kennels in Picklewick and I've got Bertie with me.'

There was a loud huff on the other end of the line, followed by, 'It didn't take *her* long to decide she couldn't cope with him, did it? Well, I'm going to tell you what I told her – I don't want him. He's too much trouble. If she hadn't said she'd have him, I'd have taken him to the sanctuary soon, anyway.'

Jakob was having difficulty following her. 'I'm sorry, I don't understand. *Who* can't cope with him?'

'My uncle's neighbour, Gretta.' Erica sounded impatient. 'When she brought him back yesterday, she said she wanted him. Seems she's changed her mind.'

Jakob was still confused. 'Are you telling me she brought him back, then took him away with her?'

'Said she'd have him. I agreed as it saved me having to hand him over to you lot, especially since I've got my uncle's house to sort out. I was just about to drive over there, in fact; my son has arranged for a clearance company to come in today and he's there supervising.'

'You were going to take him to *the sanctuary*?' Jakob said, needing to check he hadn't misheard.

'That's right.' More impatience. 'Didn't she tell you?'

'No.' He wondered why, but that was quickly followed by the realisation that Gretta must be going frantic.

The next number he called was hers, but when there was no reply, it occurred to him that if she was working she may have turned her phone off, and if that was indeed the case, she mightn't even be aware that Bertie had escaped.

'Maisie, can you hold the fort for a while?' he asked. 'I've just found Bertie in the lane and I need to take him back to Gretta.'

'Bertie? Doesn't he belong to the old man's niece now?'

'He did, but she doesn't want him, so Gretta agreed to have him.'

'I thought she was here to foster a dog because she missed him? That's what she told me.'

Jakob blinked. 'When did she tell you that?'

'Yesterday. I showed her the puppies because you were on the phone to Dawn. Didn't you speak to her?'

'No,' he said slowly. 'I didn't. What time was this?'

'Around twelve, I think.'

Jakob didn't say anything: he was too busy thinking back to yesterday. Twelve was when Clare had arrived at the kennels...

It probably wasn't relevant, he decided, but even as he thought it, he had a feeling it might be.

'BERTIE? BERTIE!' Gretta had been calling him for ages and with each passing second her worry grew. Where on earth could he be? She'd searched the house and the garden, and was currently in Mr Butler's house, having also scoured his garden without success.

The issue she had was that Mr Butler's house was being emptied by two burly men and one slim, bearded one, who seemed to be overseeing matters.

'Are you sure you haven't seen him?' she begged. 'He used to live here.'

'So you said,' one of them replied.

'Might he have got into the van?' It was half full already, and she feared he might have jumped into it and become trapped, or was lying low because...

Her heart went out to him. His home was being dismantled in front of his very eyes. No wonder the poor little thing didn't want to be found.

'Can you check again?' she pleaded. 'He's got to be here somewhere.' She didn't want to think about the alternative, that he might not be here at all and that he'd run off. But where could he have run to?

Gretta highly doubted he would have gone back to Erica.

No, he had to be here somewhere. He *had* to.

Then she heard it – his familiar bark – and she sagged with relief. 'Bertie, where are you?'

He barked again, the sound coming from the street, and she darted outside. Then skidded to a halt because, standing in front of her house with Bertie at his feet, was Jakob.

'There you are!' she cried, hurrying over to the dog and crouching down. Bertie tried to scramble onto her lap. 'Where have you been, you naughty boy? I've been looking everywhere for you.'

Jakob said, 'I tried phoning, but there wasn't any answer, so I thought I'd bring him straight here in case you were working and hadn't heard your phone.'

She had her face buried in Bertie's fur but looked up when she realised what he'd said. 'Bring him? *You* found him?' To her dismay and annoyance, desire flared inside her when she met his gaze, and she chewed her lip.

'I did. He was on Muddypuddle Lane.'

'What was he doing *there?*' Gretta was incredulous.

'No idea. I rang Erica Hilliard, and she told me that Bertie is yours now.'

'Er, that's right.' She felt awkward, thinking that perhaps she should have let Jakob know.

She straightened up. Damn, it was good to see him. He looked tired, although she refused to think why that could be, as an image of him and the woman from the supermarket popped into her head. Best not to think about that.

Jakob was looking at the men hoisting an old-fashioned sideboard onto the van.

'They're clearing Mr Butler's house,' she explained. 'I think it's upset him.'

'I expect it has. I'm not sure why he headed to Muddypuddle Lane, though. Get off, Bertie,' he added, as the dog tugged at his jeans with his teeth.

'I don't suppose we'll ever know,' Gretta said. 'Bertie, leave Jakob alone.' Her eyes met Jakob's. 'Thanks for bringing him back.'

'Do you need any help making the garden more secure?' he asked.

Stiffly, Gretta replied, 'I can manage, thanks.' Assuming they were done, she reached down to grab her dog, who was still holding onto the bottom of Jakob's jeans for dear life. 'Let go, Bertie,' she commanded, trying to prise his jaws open.

He let out a playful growl and gave her the side-eye.

'This isn't a game,' she told him. 'You've got plenty of toys in the house.'

The situation was getting embarrassing. Gretta was far too close to Jakob for comfort. Being this near to him was doing all sorts of odd things to her insides.

Considering Jakob was the expert on dogs, she fully expected him to put his expertise to good use and intervene, but he simply stood there, and when she glanced up, she found him studying her with a strange expression.

He said, 'Maisie tells me you were at The Forever Home yesterday.'

Oh, God, had he seen her spying on him? Heat swept into her cheeks and she knew she was blushing. 'I was thinking about fostering a dog, but now that I've got Bertie back...' She ground to a halt.

He was still looking at her oddly. 'You left without speaking to me,' he said, and she knew she'd been rumbled.

'I saw you,' she muttered.

'Was I with a woman?'

'Yes.'

He closed his eyes. When he opened them again, there was an intensity in them that stole her breath. 'You've been honest with me about your past. I need to tell you about mine,' he said, then glanced up at the men who were now taking a breather on the tailgate of the van. 'Not here, though. Can I come in?'

'Okay, sure.' She had doubts about this, hoping he wasn't going to do an 'I like you, but...' speech. Seeing him snogging another woman was enough explanation, thank you. She'd got the message and didn't need him to mansplain.

Bertie was happy though, finally releasing his hold on the jeans, leaving a slobbery stain on them.

Gretta wasn't in the mood to offer Jakob a cosy cup of coffee (her heart was still thumping from the scare of losing Bertie – and from seeing Jakob unexpectedly) so once inside, she turned to him, folded her arms and said, 'What is it you want to tell me?'

Taking a deep breath, he seemed to gather himself. 'The woman at the kennels was my ex-fiancée, Clare. I haven't seen her since we split up three years ago.'

'There's no need to explain,' she said – she didn't want to hear it.

'Hear me out, please? When you say you *saw* me, I'm assuming you saw Clare kissing me?'

Gretta looked away and twitched her eyebrows in acknowledgement.

'It wasn't what it seemed,' he said.

Oh yeah? she thought. 'Look, it's none of my business who you kiss—'

'I want to kiss *you.*'

'You're *joking.*' Gretta's mouth dropped open.

'I'm not, I—'

 'You're in love with *another woman* and you want to kiss *me*?' She was flabbergasted at the cheek of it and extremely disappointed in him. She'd thought he was a better man than that.

'I'm not in love with Clare.' His gaze was open and direct, and incredibly intense.

'But you were kissing her!' she pointed out, furiously.

'What you saw was *her* kissing *me*. I wasn't actually taking part.'

'She was all over you!'

'She was, but not for long. Not when she realised I wasn't interested.'

Gretta was conflicted. Should she mention the conversation she'd overheard? No, she didn't think she would. She didn't want to get involved.

He soldiered on. 'I loved her once – heart and soul – but she betrayed me with my best friend. She'd been unfaithful before and I'd forgiven her; but I could never forgive her for that, especially since she left me for him. I don't know what went wrong between them and I don't care. She might be back in Thornbury, but she's not back in my life. For three years I've been too scared to let anyone get close – until you.'

'*Me?*' Gretta blinked.

'You don't have to say anything, and I don't expect you to feel the same way. I just wanted to explain.'

'The same way? What way is that?' Her heart was beating so fast she feared it would explode, and a nervous excitement was building in her stomach.

'I'm falling for you, Gretta.' His voice was matter of fact, but his eyes were haunted.

When she said nothing, his shoulders sagged and he nodded. 'It's okay. I'm glad you've got Bertie back. See you around.'

Bertie, hearing his name, whined. He was looking from her to Jakob and back again, and Gretta could have sworn he had a disbelieving look on his face. When he let out a loud bark, she jumped.

It cut through her inertia and she suddenly realised she had a decision to make, one which would affect the rest of her life.

Could she trust again? Could she bring herself to give her heart to this man, because if she couldn't there was no point in even contemplating a relationship with him.

The problem was, she suspected she already had. Jakob had sneaked into her heart as effectively as Bertie.

It didn't alter the fact that she was scared: love made people vulnerable and she *hated* feeling vulnerable. If you loved someone there was a chance they could hurt you – as she'd found out to her cost. If she let Jakob in, she'd be taking a leap of faith.

Was she ready for that?

Gretta took a deep breath *and leapt.*

'Wait. Don't go.'

He halted in the doorway and slowly turned around. Hope lit up his face, yet he made no move towards her, as he said, 'I won't hurt you, Gretta. When I love someone, I love them wholeheartedly and with everything I've got.'

He was telling the truth. Her certainty was absolute; just as she was certain that Bertie had entered her life to show her how to love again.

Actually, she suspected that the dog might have had something to do with Jakob being here now... He certainly looked very pleased with himself.

Gretta recognised that she would have to make the next move. Jakob was as wary and as vulnerable as she, and he'd already revealed more of himself than she guessed he was comfortable with.

Slowly, uncertainly, she took a step towards him.

His eyes never left her face.

She took another. And another.

Then his mouth was on hers, and she was swept into his embrace.

As he kissed her, her fear dissipated, replaced by passion and the conviction that she, like Bertie, had found her forever home.

CHAPTER SEVENTEEN

THE BED WAS A snuggle pile of two humans, three dogs and a cat. The cat was in charge, naturally. The humans indulged her, and the dogs merely did as she told them.

Gretta opened one sleepy eye and sighed contentedly. She couldn't feel her right leg because there was seventy pounds of golden retriever lying on it. And lying half on and half off Stan, was Ripley, who was snoring loudly. Bertie was sprawled on Jakob's bare chest, whilst Zaza had appropriated Gretta's pillow. Luckily, Jakob's chest was broad enough to accommodate both her head and Bertie's stocky body.

She wasn't as comfortable as she could be, but she was too contented to move. *This is what Sunday mornings are all about*, she thought happily, *lazing in bed*. They didn't happen often though, because Jakob didn't have a nine to five, Monday to Friday job. And neither did she. Gretta had got into the habit of working when he did and being off when he was.

Without opening his eyes, he said, 'I'll make us some brunch in a minute, then we should take the dogs for a walk.'

'Not just yet,' she pleaded.

He craned his neck, bending his head to kiss her on the nose. 'Lazy bones.'

'*Happy* bones,' she replied.

There was something rather wonderful about the whole family snuggling together in her bed – and the animals were *definitely* part of her family. Mind you, they hadn't slept in her bedroom last night, and pretty soon she was going to turf them out again because she had some unfinished business with Jakob...

For the moment though, she was happy to snuggle, revelling in the love surrounding her.

In the three months since she and Jakob had become an item, she'd grown to love his dogs as much as he, and in return they'd bonded with her. Which was a good job, since he spent nearly all his free time at her place, and she minded the dogs for him when he was at work. All except for Trixie, who had been adopted by Jakob's parents and was now living her best life with them in the motor home they'd recently acquired since his mum had retired.

Everything had fallen into place perfectly, as though it was meant to be, but in her quieter and more reflective moments, Gretta had a sneaky suspicion that much of it had been engineered by a certain French bulldog who was currently snuffling in her ear. Not only had Bertie found his forever home, but he'd ensured that Gretta had found hers, and she would be eternally grateful to the little dog.

'I love you,' she whispered to him, without thinking.

Jakob tensed, and Gretta froze. Oh hell, she'd been talking to Bertie, and now Jakob thought...

'I love you, too,' he whispered back, then turned onto his side, spilling Bertie off his chest and onto the bed.

It was as she was about to confess that she'd hadn't been speaking to *him*, that she realised it was true, that she *did* love Jakob – with all her heart.

'Out,' she told the animals, kicking the door shut with an outstretched foot after they begrudgingly obliged.

It was time to show this remarkable man just how much she loved him, and as she reached for him, joy lit her from within.

Gretta had found true love at last.

ACKNOWLEDGEMENTS

There are always so many who deserve to be thanked, that I rarely know where to start.

This time, I do, and I'll begin by thanking the wonderful dogs I've been honoured to share my life with. Their devotion, love, and loyalty has left their paw prints not only on my heart, but on my very soul. And I can't forget the cats, either. They love equally deeply, but in their own way...

Now for the humans.

Thanks to my family, especially my parents who finally gave in to my incessant nagging to buy me a dog. I was eleven and Sally was my shadow. Long gone now, but never, *ever* forgotten. She was a cocker spaniel, and the sweetest, most loving—

Oh, yes, I was supposed to be thanking *people*, wasn't I?

Try again...

Thanks to my husband for not objecting (too much) when I disappeared for an afternoon and came back with a Westie puppy...

Humans – okay, got it.

Where was I? Oh, yes, my family... You know who you are. Thank you for everything, and especially to Poppy for making me smile. Every. Single. Day. And for the ecstatic greeting when I walk into a room (even if I've only been upstairs), and for the wet kisses and the comforting paw...

People!!

Catherine Mills deserves my thanks, as always. Not just for pointing out glaring plot holes, but for her unwavering support.

Valerie Brown, who reads faster than anyone else on the planet, and her eye for detail is second to none – you have my continued gratitude.

Back to my family again, I love you all, whether you have fur or not.

Last, but most importantly, you, my readers, because you make this crazy writing lark worthwhile! *Thank you.*

There are loads more large print books in the Muddypuddle Lane series. Available at all good book stores, or ask your local library.

About Etti

Etti Summers is the author of wonderfully romantic fiction with happy ever afters guaranteed.

She is also a wife, a mum, a pink gin enthusiast, a veggie grower and a keen reader.

www.ingramcontent.com/pod-product-compliance
Lightning Source LLC
Chambersburg PA
CBHW070819190726
48292CB00006B/2053